DALIT KOTHA

The Subaltern Voice in a
Bengali Woman's Narratives

AF655761

DALIT KOTHA

The Subaltern Voice in a Bengali Woman's Narratives

MANJU BALA

Translators

Tarik Anowar

Saddam Saikh

AUTHORSPRESS

Worldwide Circulation through Authorspress Global Network
First Published in 2022
by
Authorspress
Q-2A Hauz Khas Enclave, New Delhi-110 016 (India)
Phone: (0) 9818049852
E-mail: authorspressgroup@gmail.com
Website: www.authorspressbooks.com

Dalit Kotha: The Subaltern Voice in a Bengali Woman's Narratives

ISBN 978-93-5529-370-1

Copyright © 2022 Manju Bala

Translators: Tarik Anowar, Saddam Saikh

All rights reserved. No part of this book may be reproduced or transmitted in any form or by any means, electronic, mechanical, photocopying, or otherwise, without the express written consent of the author.

Printed in India by Manipal Technologies Limited, Manipal

Foreword

It is indeed a pleasure to write the 'Foreword' for this volume. The book comes as one more valuable addition to the field of Dalit literature.

Dalit writings have today come of age. Their identity as a separate stream in literature is today well established. It was indeed a hard struggle for Dalit writers to gain the attention that they now enjoy. They were for long criticized from the angle of dominant mainstream literature on grounds that they did not meet the standards of literary aesthetics. Their ideas were gross, the language was rough, and the finesse was absent. Yes, the allegations were largely true. Dalit writings very often lacked the refinement of non-Dalit literature. And, that was because the works reflected the realities of Dalit existence, the lived-in experiences of the downtrodden – the hard, existence thrust upon them by mainstream Hindu Brahminical society for centuries. How could the realistic writings exude elegance of the manner expected of them? As such, Dalit writings have claimed and created their own aesthetics, demanded recognition of their own-defined style, eroded the basis of criticisms leveled against their essence and established their presence.

Maharashtra led the way. The spread of education, pressure of the Dalit movement and struggles against the prevailing conditions of existence, inspired a section of Dalit youths to take up cultural and literary tools to express their aversion for and anger against existing inequality and the repressive social order. It was through their efforts that there had emerged an altogether new genre of protest literature. Dalit literature. Inspired by the ideas of Ambedkar, Marx and the Black Panther Movement of the USA, it established itself through the Dalit Panther Movement of the 1970s.

Pioneering work in the field of Dalit literature in Maharashtra, set in motion a whole chain of Dalit writings thereafter, in different languages and in different parts of the country. In the same tradition, despite a lag of a couple of decades, since the 1990s Bangla Dalit writings were inspired into becoming a part of that identity. One after the other enthusiastic Dalit writers came up with their contributions to enrich the fund of Bangla Dalit literature and build up a 'movement'. On the one hand, they wrote new pieces with new levels of consciousness, on the other they retrieved what already existed but was scattered, virtually forgotten and lost over years. Soon, what developed was no less than a treasure. It was a vibrant movement to create, re-create and reclaim. Drawing inspiration from the Dalit literary movement of Maharashtra, Dalit writers writing in Bangla built their own organisational networks such as the Bangla Dalit Sahitya Sanstha, published their own little magazines and set up their publishing units to carry forward their movement. They were determined not to be cowed down in their efforts by the lack of cooperation and cold behavior meted out by upper caste writers of fame, mainstream literary bodies and publishing houses. They needed the space, and they were building their own. Enthusiastic Dalit writers pushed their way from invisibility to visibility. Noted amongst them have been writers like Manohar Mouli Biswas, Kapil Krishna Thakur, Jatin Bala, Nitish Biswas, Raju Das, Dhurjoti Naskar, Bimalendu Haldar.

The creations of Bangla Dalit writers cover the widest of range of literature, spanning from fiction to non-fiction. Through their writings, they depict their lived experiences, their pains, their sorrows, their hopes. These are reflected in autobiographies, novels, poems, plays and short stories. It is perhaps the short stories that are most popular, most numerous and the best articulated amongst their writings. In most cases they reflect the realities of existence of the most lowly, seen from a participant point of view. Such stories are hardly just stories, they are more than that. In their physical and historical settings they reveal uniqueness of presentation. The story-tellers' own lived –in experiences very often merge with those of the characters in the tales.

In the field of Bangla Dalit literature, Dalit women's voices are lesser heard than those of their male counterparts. This is hardly surprising. Dalit women still lag behind the men of their communities in terms of literacy. Further, the burden of daily domestic chores and the hurdles of patriarchal norms tend to work as impediments to their creative writings. While they significantly contribute to the carrying ahead of oral literature in the form of folk music and folk tales, those using the pen have been few in number. Yet, when they write, they make their mark of distinction. Kalyani

Thakur Charal, Manju Bala, Puspa Bairagya, Lily Halder and Smritikana Howladar are among the frontline women writers contributing to Bangla Dalit literature today. They write, and they write with a difference. Through their writings they critique the established caste norms, class exploitation as well as patriarchal values. Like other Dalit writers, they dare to tread the paths of the different genres of Dalit literature.

Manju Bala, born in 1954, a graduate having a close association with Bangla Dalit Sahitya Sanstha, has emerged as a powerful voice of Dalit women writers. Among her writings, her short stories have been particularly impressive. They reflect the voice not just of a Dalit writer, but a Dalit feminist writer; one who, through her pen, exposes the hard realities of life that Dalit women face – the dual oppressions of caste and gender. A translated collection of some of her Bangla short stories in English, as is presented in this volume, would surely draw the attention of readers interested in the field, but unfamiliar with the Bangla language. It will establish that not only are Dalit women writing in Bangla, but they are writing well!

Dated: 28.2.2022
Place: Kolkata

Debi Chatterjee
Retd Professor
Department of International Relations
Jadavpur University
Kolkata
And
Editor
Contemporary Voice of Dalit

Chaturtha Dunia

Bangla Dalit Sahitya Sanstha was formed in 1992 after the sad immolation of Chuni Kotal, a tribal girl of Goaldihi village of West Medinipore while she was doing her masters in Anthropology in Vidyasagar University, West Bengal. It happened due to caste hatred inside the class room and even in the campus outside class room from some particular teacher. Protest rally was organised in Kolkata and even in the university campus. In consequence of the incident a literary organisation of creativity and activism took its shape which ultimately opened a window to publish their own writings as well. This publishing window is "Chaturtha Dunia" and the same window that published the book of short stories "Chora Bali" means 'Treacherous Sand' written by Manju Bala.

The BDSS has their mission to set up a casteless and classless society without any discrimination amongst humankind. Their motto is to9 work for their own agendas such as (1) The writer shall hold the torch of liberation and shall participate in people's movements. (2) On the social front they are against the casteism, communalism, fundamentalism and all kinds of inequality based on birth and sex. (3) On economic front they are against the feudalism and capitalism. (3) On political front they are against feudalism and capitalism. (4) On cultural front they are to demolish the cultural hegemony and (5) On literary front they are to depict the marginality of the dalit life.

Manju Bala's book of short stories 'Treacherous Sand' shall give pleasure and loveliness to stand for the new social outlook.

Manahar Mouli Biswas
Editor: Chaturtha Dunia.

The Author's Note

I congratulate the translators on their efforts in translating *Dalit Kotha: The Subaltern Voice in a Bengali Woman's Narratives* into English. The contribution of this translation would broaden the scope of Bengali Dalit literature, particularly the discourse of Dalit women. Almost every story in this collection shows how Dalits in Bengal endure caste discrimination at various phases of their life.

The Bengali social system, like that of the rest of India, is built on caste hierarchy. The anti-caste movement in Bengal was started by two renowned social reformers, Harichand Thakur and Guruchand Thakur, before Babasaheb Ambedkar. Bengali lower caste people staged a large protest in 1911 to change their negative identify, *Chandal*, and rename their caste designation Namashudras. The ongoing caste movement was disrupted by colonial Bengal's partition, and they became a rootless, displaced, and misplaced group. They reassembled their lives in the post-partition period and, beginning in 1992, reignited the anti-caste campaign through literary and social resistance.

This book is crucial for understanding how caste and gender function as dominant institutions in the Bengali social system. In West Bengal, Dalit pupils are referred to as *Sonar Chand* and *Sonar Tukra* because they are given reservation privileges due to their low social position. Upper-caste colleagues and friends frequently dispute the merit and capability of Dalits in academic institutions. Dalit women are subjected to more oppression than Dalit men. Chuni Kotal's tragic death serves as stark proof in this regard. The *Bhadralok* stopped her from pursuing higher education, forcing her to commit suicide. The upper caste *Bhadralok* would rather have Dalit women working as housemaids and Dalit males working as day labourers than seeing them in academic, political, or administrative positions.

Bengali Dalit literature began as a social and literary movement to expose and oppose caste-based injustice in Bengal, based on the ideologies of Harichand Thakur, Guruchand Thakur, and Babasaheb

Ambedkar. This work, *Dalit Kotha: The Subaltern Voice in a Bengali Woman's Narratives* was written with the same goal of changing society and valuing basic human values.

Manju Bala

Dalit Literature

The term *Dalit* literally stands for 'Crushed' or 'broken' and basically represents the masses who are suppressed and oppressed in the society. In the post-Independent India, this word gained popularity while representing the Shudras, the lowest caste in the Hindu social hierarchal system. The invader Aryans were the predecessor of today's Brahmins who effortlessly overpowered the indigenous Dravidian tribes with their unique military system and they converted the original inhabitants to permanent slaves under their authority. The Brahmins stratified the society into four categories on the basis of profession and secured for themselves the topnotch position to control over others. The religious scriptures like Vedas, Shastrasand shrutis etc., were composed by them as a mechanism to hold the power and control the society for time eternal. In Manusmriti, the Dalits have been designated as untouchables, the most-lowly caste on the earth. Today, they are addressed with different nomenclatures in different parts of India such as Paraiyas, Uchalya, Mahar, Chandalas, Namashudras, Scheduled Caste and the list further continues. They were ostracised from the mainstream society and their basic rights were taken away at different levels such as the society, religion, education, economy and politics. Thus, the Dalits have been suffering from identity crisis and other basic rights since time immemorial.

Dalit literature is written by the Dalit writers on the various subjects of Dalit with their Dalit consciousness. The journey of Dalit literary movement started in Maharashtra around the year 1960s. And then gradually, this literary trend started emerging in diverse vernacular languages in other parts of India too. This literary movement has been greatly influenced by the philosophical and revolutionary thoughts and ideals of Babasaheb Ambedkar. Some contemporary remarkable Dalit writers are notably – Sharan Kumar Limbale, Daya Pawar, Laxmane Gaikwade, Laxman Mane, Baburao Bagul, Omprakash Valmiki, Kancha Illaiah, Narendra Jadav and so on. Dalit literature evolved as a stiff resistance against the inhuman practice of caste discrimination. Through their literary discourse,

Dalit authors relook and rewrite the history of their ancestors and their harrowed inhuman experiences that they encountered under the Brahminical domination.

Dalit literature is the representation of the suffering and exploitation of the Dalits by the upper castes who wield total influence in the society. Dalit writers believe that their literature specifically highlights the social issues and simply bypass the elements of beauty and romance. Dalit writers claim their literature is distinctive from the mainstream literature as it aims to eradicate the social evils and not to provide romantic flavour to the readers.

Dalit literature systematically avoids the mainstream literary aestheticism. According to the Dalit writers, their painful experiences belong to the realm of truth which is beautiful and this lofty image of grief is subject matter of their writings. Although the mainstream writers include the Dalits as subaltern class but they hardly deal with the caste issues in their writings. Some renowned writers like Arundhati Roy, Mulk Raj Anand, Manik Bandyopadhyay, Rabindranath Tagore etc. have given sufficient space to Dalits in their writings from their observation or from their sympathetic perspective. Their depiction of the Dalits is sometimes arbitrary based on their imagination which do not express the real struggle of the Dalits. On the contrary, the Dalit writers write from their personal experiences portraying the true colour of the Dalit lives. They generally write their literature in the vernacular languages which reveals the true spirit of their society.

The Dalit female writers like Bama, Urmila Pawar, Shantabai Kamble, Baby Kamble, Meena Kandasamy, P Sivakami and so many who have drawn special attention to how Dalit women are doubly oppressed as women and as Dalit women. Under the abject poverty, Dalit women also need to work outside their house. They often become the victims of sexual violence at the work places. The so-called upper castes consider the Dalits as untouchables and sometimes harass the Dalit women to gratify their sexual lust. The events like abduction, rape and breach of Dalit women's chastity by the upper caste Hindus have become the daily news. Many a times, the Dalit women workers are not paid duly according to their work. The Dalit women narratives explore how Dalit women are exploited inside and outside of their houses.

Dalit literature bears a great resemblance to African American Literature. It can rightly be said that Indian dalits have been greatly influenced by the African-American black literature. As the blacks were treated as slaves by the American white people, similarly the Indian Dalits were also treated as slaves by the upper castes Hindus. The only difference between the two is that racism is the social construct and untouchability in India is deeply rooted into religious scriptures. Like African-American writers, the Indian Dalit writers deprecate the discrimination, oppression and inequalities through their writings.

One of the central objectives of Dalit literature is to make the Dalit community aware about their marginal social status and inspires and empowers the Dalits to fight against this age-old slavery. Dalit literature is a kind of revolutionary movement to bring about a change in the society. It seeks to dismantle all forms of prejudices like untouchability, discrimination and exploitation from the society. The Dalit activists and the writers aim to form a society where all people are treated as equal and free from all sorts of discriminations.

Earlier the Bengali Dalits were known as Chandal, an untouchable community. In 1911, they proclaimed the identity of their community as 'Namashudra' after running a devoted protest movement under the leadership of Guruchand Thakur. In the pre-partition Bengal, most of the Namashudras used to reside in East Bengal (Now Bangladesh). Bengali Namashudras formed a new religious movement called 'Matua' a separate religious entity under the leadership of Guruchand Thakur and his son Harichand Thakur. This religion was created as a protest against inhuman practices by the Brahmins. These Matuas neither followed the commandments of Vedas nor customs and traditions of the upper caste Hindus.

The partition of Colonial Bengal not only dismantled their political domination but also made them destitute refugees in West Bengal. In the post partition West Bengal, the question of caste was overpowered by the discourse of class. The mainstream political leaders of West Bengal discouraged and defamed the dalit leaders like Jogendranath Mandal who tried to bring the Dalits together by raising the caste issues. The lamentable experience of Bengali Dalit refugees in camps in Bengal and in Dandakaranya and the government-sponsored massacre of the Dalits in Marichjhapi remained as unwritten chapters till the development of Bengali Dalit literature.

In West Bengal, Dalit literary movement developed much later in compare to Marathi, Tamil and Hindi linguistic background. Actually, as a means of social activism. Jyotiba Phule and BR Ambedkar helped awaken social conscience by focusing on education, union and social activism.

However, Dalit women failed to raise their issues forcefully on any significant platform, especially Bengali Dalit women treated as untouchable among untouchables. Their feeble voice was muffled by the combined forces of patriarchy and casteism. Manju Bala, through her tales, attempts to vocalise their concern and untold suffering. In Bala's stories, the issue of caste and gender are inextricably connected to bring to the surface the mechanism of oppression that underline all human relationships, motherhood, sexual alliances, educational and career opportunities.

As a Dalit feminist voice, Bala attacks the so-called progressive and educated people blindfolded by belief in casteism and patriarchy. She underlines their hypocrisy through many tales translated in this book. Medical science explains that male chromosomes are responsible for the birth of males or females nor women. However, this information does not stop educated Arnababu from divorcing Renu as she could not beget a male heir in the tale "The Yolk". He speaks incessantly about gender equality, women's liberation and empowerment at public platforms but appear a male chauvinist and practice gender discrimination at home. Manata Ganguli is a college teacher, and Jeet is a doctor. However, both seem enslaved by caste hegemony in "The Inequality". Mamta constantly reminds her daughter in law Phulia that she belongs to the scheduled caste through her behaviour and action. Even Jeet, through his silence, collaborate in the practice of caste hegemony. Bijoy Sanal added a new definition of liberation and egalitarian ideology through his writing but refused to marry his daughter to a Muslim boy in the story "Quicksand". Shefali and the whole neighbourhood of Mukesh and Mala reveal their casteist mentality in accusing Thumpa of being the mother of an illegally begotten child based on her lower caste belonging in the same story. In contrast, the child's mother was an upper-caste woman Shashoti.

Renuka is a school teacher who becomes an agency of caste oppression and gender violence with her doctor son Kalyan in "The Conflict". She indulges in physical violence in imparting lessons of subservience to her daughter in law Banani, a lower caste woman. These stories show that education fails to liberate the mind of these higher caste people who are victims of gender politics and caste hegemony.

Bala highlights the structure of oppression and injustice and which undermine humanitarian values. Her story "Realisation" emphasises prioritising humanity over religious fanaticism. The narrative of Joriya exudates the lesson of female empowerment and independence.

Some tales are contemporary in themes. "The Paw" discusses the evil impact of industrialisation on the rural economy in the vested interest of politicians. "Topsy Turvy" shows the negative aspect of modernisation at the cost of Indian family values. However, most of them are female-centric deal with caste and gender sensibilities.

The story "Cancer" takes a bitter dig at the cattiest mentality where a maths teacher Sukanta is not allowed to teach his subject as he belongs to the scheduled caste and talents is a monopoly of the upper caste. Despite his love marriage with Tithi, she never leaves an opportunity to humiliate her husband as she is always conscious of her higher caste identity. The title itself points out that casteism is the canker of Indian society, a deadly disease that needs immediate intervention and treatment. The story "Realisation" celebrates humanity over religious orthodoxy and casteist mentality. It also commemorates female empowerment through Joriya's character.

Instead of simply protesting against social discrimination, injustice her tales celebrate the undaunting spirit, incessant struggle and courage of women Parul in "Ups and down" and Banani in "The Conflict" and Ketaki in "The Special Maid". Parul is sexually exploited by her master's son but dares to bring her child into the world without any support. Stories like "Friend" endorse real female empowerment and a progressive mindset. The story of Saro in "Brain wash" salutes the indomitable spirit of a woman who is illiterate but wants to educate her son. These representative females refuse to submit in front of coercive forces of society and try to redefine their lives on the line of self-respect, dignity, assertion, and liberation.

Prof. Rubina Iqbal
Dept of English
AMU, Aligarh

Manju Bala, A Bengali Dalit Woman Writer

Manju Bala is one of the emerging writers in the Bengali Dalit literary world. She is a Dalit feminist as well as an activist who has been fighting for the rights of the women of the marginalised section since a very long time. Her parents migrated from East Pakistan (now Bangladesh) to Calcutta where the writer was born in 1948 during the partition of colonial Bengal. She completed her entire education in Calcutta, a famous metropolis and commercial hub of West Bengal. She penned a plethora of books which are notably – *Osharohir Opekkhai* (Waiting for the Horse-rider), *Churno Somudrer Dhew* 2013 (Waves of Shattered Sea), *Chothurtho Bishwer Chitrolekha* 2017, (The Portrait of the Fourth World), *Chorabali* (Quicksand), *Uttoran* (The Ascension) and so on. She also started a magazine named *Akhon Takhon* (Now and Then) since 1997 to publish and propagate the Dalit writings and to protest against the ills of casteism and racial discrimination prevalent in Bengal. Her writings are basically centred around the pains and sufferings of the lower caste people victimised under the domination of the upper caste *Bhadralok*. She is the seer for the lower caste people who struggle hard to annihilate the stigma of casteism and desperately search for their human identity.

Bengali Dalit women writings frame a new literary canon in India. The Dalit women are the worst victims of caste, class and gender in the Indian social framework. The gruesome reports of verbal abuse, abduction, molestation, human trafficking, rape and murder and other forms of physical and mental harassment abound in the daily headlines of newspapers. They are often harassed and mistreated inside as well as outside of their house.

Dalit women writings bring to the fore all sorts of issues that are absent and sometimes misrepresented in the mainstream narratives. The Indian feminists too do not truly recognise the pain and trauma of the women pertaining to the lower caste background. They conspicuously avert the discussion on gender and caste and maintain complete silence on these social issues. A similar catastrophic situation can be noticed in the lives of African-American black women to a considerable level.

As a Dalit woman writer, Manju Bala has beautifully shown her expertise in the domain of essays, short stories and poetry to address the question of caste, class and gender. Her writings are the authentic testimonies of the issues basically rooted in caste and gender. Despite focusing on the elegance of literary aestheticism, her works underscore the truthful portrayal of predicaments that every Dalit undergoes in his/her day-to-day life. In the post-partition epoch, her contribution has given a new dimension and brought about a revolution in the Bengali literary movement. The subject matter of her writings displays many commonalities with Bama, Daya Pawar and other women writers in other vernacular languages. She has been greatly influenced by the revolutionary ideas of Lord Buddha, Harichand Thakur, Guruchand Thakur and the philosophy of Babasaheb Ambedkar.

Her short story book *Chorabali* translated as *Dalit Kotha: The Subaltern Voice in a Bengali Woman's Narratives,* is a socio-political representation of Bengali society that seeks to break the so-called *Bhadralok's* myth that caste does not matter in Bengal. Her narratives showcase that Bengali Dalits are victimized mostly verbally and psychologically rather than physical assault. This is the main cause for the absence of caste questions in West Bengal which is quite difficult to understand it from outside. Therefore, it should not be considered that Bengal is a casteless society. Bala narrates how the *Bhadralok* Bengalis often humiliate and scoff at the STs by calling them as 'Sonar Tukra' (piece of gold) and the SCs as the 'Sonar Chand' (golden moon). They disdain the ST and SC teachers and students by labelling them as the product of reservation quotas and therefore, they are less meritorious. The *Bhadralok* often raise question on the skills and merits of the Dalits. Bala claims that the upper caste wants the Dalits to work as labourers and farmers in the fields rather than utilise their intelligence in the academic field. In her short story *Jhi Special* (The Special Maid), she narrates the identity crisis of a lower caste maid in Bengali society. The Dalit maid Ketoki has been expelled from her job by the house mistress on account of her inability to work one day due to her son's illness. The house mistress accused her as a liar and debarred her from the job pushing her into the state of starvation. The identity crisis of Dalit refugees in the post-Partition West Bengal creates a distinctive historiography that has remained oblivious erstwhile in the mainstream writings. The discussion of women's issues in the male-dominated Bengali society provides an alternative reading to Manju Bala's narratives.

Her poetry *Osharohir Opekkhai* and *Churno Somudrer Dhew (2013)* are important contributions to the development of Bengali Dalit feminist discourse. Her poetry not only echoes the agonies of the Dalits but also serves as a kind of weapon through which she articulates the revolutionary ideas to bring about a change in the society. Her poems are characteristically symbolic in nature and deeply rooted in socio-economic and socio-religious contexts. In her poem *Ar Niche Nambo Na* (I shall not go gown anymore), Bala has successfully vivified the prevalence of caste prejudice in the contemporary Bengal. The verse reveals that during a short ride in an autorickshaw, a *Bhadramohila* (upper caste woman) meets a good-looking girl and offers her to be her daughter-in-law. During the conversation with her, the upper caste woman comes to know that the girl belongs to the Namashudra community, a lower caste in Bengal. So, she decides not to proceed with any further discussion in this matter. This is how Manju Bala, as a keen social observer, has authentically portrayed the issue of caste and untouchability in the present-day West Bengal. In a nutshell, it can be said that her style of poetry expresses the hopes and despair of the subaltern people.

Apart from writing short stories and poetry, Manju Bala has also published a book of essays entitled *Chothurtho Bishwer Chitrolekha* 2017 (The Portrait of the Fourth World) which serves as a unique masterpiece to channelise Dalit literary discourse. Her essays grapple with multiple aspects like the origin and development of Dalit literature, philosophical ideas of Ambedkar, Harichand and Guruchand Thakur and the socio-political status of the Dalit women in the Indian societal framework. The discussion of her essays on multifarious aspects provides an alternative reading to the Dalit literary world.

As an emerging Bengali Dalit woman writer, her writings provide a strong sense of subaltern perspective. It is very imperative to consider that her writings consciously form a new method of resistance. There is always a sense of rebellion and revolutionary temperament in her writings against the hegemony of evil forces in society. She has highlighted as to how the Dalit women are doubly marginalised on the grounds of caste and gender. As a representative of the Dalit women, Manju Bala encourages other Dalit women to raise a voice of dissent against the tyrannic forces for claiming their identity and basic rights. Breaking the chain of the age-old caste system, she dreams of forming a society that assures freedom, equality and justice for all.

Tarik Anowar

Contents

1

Ups and Downs

Saddam Saikh

Strings of small houses with wooden leafy roofs both sides of the railroad track are lined rows of tiny homes with wooden leafy roofs. It's better not to call them houses, rather huts. These huts are walled with discarded sheets of plastic, tattered sackcloth or broken bamboo fences. The doors of these huts are so small that one almost has to crawl in. Most of these people are often refugees, people of East Bengal. Leaving their home soil, they are floating in this country's sea of people like broken pieces of straw. Their livelihood comes from daily labor. Some of the men of these huts pull rickshaws, some are masons, some do small business and some are hawkers. The women do not sit around either. They wash dishes, clean the houses and cook at the upper-class households. Now they are not called maids, instead they are called domestic workers. In one of these huts, the small family of Tarak Mandal lives. So far, Tarak has nourished this family with the blood, sweat and tears of his body. He has not let Bhavani work in those upper-class households. He has admitted his elder daughter Parul in the local primary school. And the other two daughters Bakul and Chameli are still young. Tarak works as a mason. But it's not that he always gets jobs. Everyday poverty grabs a tighter hold. But still, he bites the bullet and their struggling lives go on. But in the end what happens is that tremendous gusts of wind, stronger than the storm, appear out of nowhere and bring disaster; though it did not uproot the whole tree, but certainly shook it to its core. One day Tarak begins coughing up blood. He seems to have a reoccurring fever for several days but does not pay it much attention. Having no other alternative, he works in that feverish state. He toils without complaint as long as he has any remaining strength in his body; until he couldn't anymore.

Bhavani now works as a domestic helper in those houses. Despite the doctor's diagnosis of serious tuberculosis, Tarak is optimistic that things would improve; he will recuperate and be able to care for his family once more. His body resembles a skeleton due to starvation. Lying on the bed, he observes the days passing by. The tremors cause his frail body to shake. Bhavani returns home in the evening after a long day at work. She brings leftovers, such as stale and insipid rice and half-rotten curries; week-old moldy bread dumped from her employer's office; and arid, fallen grains and crumbs obtained from the flea market. Bhavani slams the dirty bag on the ground. Her younger daughter appears out of nowhere, coated in dust up to her knees, and flips the bag upside-down. She grabs a dry piece of bread and bites into it rapidly. In the meantime, Tarak exits the room, holding his chest. He hasn't had anything to eat all day. When he sees the dry bread, his mouth waters. Bhavani extends a piece of bread to him. Tarak devours the bread with gusto. Bhavani takes a few drops of coconut oil from of the bottle and massages it into her palm, rubbing it into the middle of her head. 'I'm coming back after taking a plunge in the pond,' she adds as she snatches the torn towel dangling from the rope. 'Then I'll prepare a meal for you.' She hurriedly walks down the railway lines. The green lives aren't any less important than the lingering expressions of unrequited love here. The march of life multiplies a hundredfold in this wasteland.

It's been a few days since Bhavani found Parul a job in a wealthy family. Parul's responsibilities as a live-in maid include anything from cooking to cleaning rooms to performing errands and other domestic chores. During the day, both the master and mistress of the house go to work, and their only son Proloy lives in a neighbouring hostel. As a result, Parul spends a significant amount of time alone in the house.

People dream, they love to dream. Parul is the same way. Dream that she sees is swimming in the deep lake of her black eyes. She desires to further her studies. Her father even allows her to attend school, but she has to give up her goal and works in the inner sanctum of a *Bhadralok's* house.

'Mom, I'm sorry, but I can't do so much work here. It causes me a great deal of discomfort. Mom, please take me home.'

'We are born to suffer. Are we born to unwind like the *Bhadralok*?' Then she reassures her in a compassionate voice that 'it will be difficult at first. But everything will be alright after that.'

But that day, she was taken aback when she received the news of Parul's teenage pregnancy out of the blue, as if someone were hammering a large stone on her chest.

'Bhavani, take your daughter away. I've never seen such a brazen young lady. This is why you belong to the lower caste. You have no respect and no honour. That's why your daughter is expecting a child, and you'll be a grandmother!' In a mocking tone, Amala Devi tells her.

Bhavani stares blankly into the void. She doesn't even blink. Amala Devi, on the other hand, is well aware of the perpetrator. She threatens Parul that she wouldn't tell anyone who Proloy was. If she learns about that, it won't be good for Parul.

'Bhavani, pay attention! Take her to a hospital and get the baby aborted.' Then she pauses for a moment to consider anything before insulting Bhavani once more. 'Your daughter is so shameless and promiscuous that my son couldn't keep his mouth shut. Apart from that, my son is a man, and your daughter is a woman....' Bhavani can no longer tolerate it. 'All the difficulties will be solved if your son simply marries my daughter,' she stops her. Amala Devi did not expect to hear this. For a little moment, she is taken aback. But she moves on and rebuffs her.

'What exactly did you say? My son's wedding with your daughter? For a low-caste, you have an excessively large mouth! You have no right to say that! That is why you belong to the lower caste!' Finally, she offers her a bribe by stating, 'Take your daughter to a hospital within two-three days. I'll cover the cost of the abortion. I'll even compensate you with ten thousand rupees,' she says as she moves closer to Bhavani.

Bhavani is deafeningly quiet. She takes a few steps with her daughter on the way home.

Proloy sees Parul for the first time since the day he has returned home from hostel. Amala Devi is yet to return from her office. Amar *Babu*, Proloy's father, frequently comes home late at night. Parul is the only one in the house. Parul answers the door after Proloy rings the doorbell. Proloy has learned that a new maid has been kept in their house. As a result, seeing Parul does not surprise him.

'Isn't Parul your name?'

'Yes!' Parul responds with a bashful tone.

After that, Proloy begins returning home on a regular basis for no apparent reason. Except for Proloy and Parul, no one is home that night. For a while, there is no power. After lighting a candle, Parul sits in her chamber. Suddenly, there is a gentle knock on the door. As soon as Parul opens the door, Proloy enters the room, and the air extinguishes the candle. Proloy holds her and whispers, 'I love you Parul; I will marry you; I can't live without you,' before Parul can stop him. Proloy does not give her a chance to speak. He storms out of the room almost as fast as he came. His visits become nearly non-existent after that. Amala Devi, on the other hand, notices the changes in Parul's body.

'Who has done this to you?'

At first, Parul is hesitant to tell. But she has to do it in the end. Proloy's mother warns her not to mention Proloy's name to anyone else. It would not be good if I ever heard. Go to a hospital and abort the baby. That is my order. It has been over three months that a little child is blossoming in Parul's womb like a flower bud. Therefore, hearing the talks of abortion, Parul cries her eyes out. So, Bhavani does not force her anymore.

The clock strikes twelve o'clock. All of the slum's huts are suddenly flared up like wildfire. People are being cremated in their own beds as a result of the fire. Their terrible shouts reverberate across the air. Those who were able to escape their burnt huts have sought refuge in the empty primary school. It's because it's summer vacation time. These people had everything taken away from them: their loved ones, their houses, and their souls. Only their half-burned dark bodies remain. They have no idea where they will go after the holidays. But one thing is certain: they will no longer be permitted to ghettoise there.

Nobody knows what caused the fire or who sparked it. But Parul is aware of the situation. Proloy browbeat her on the street a few days ago and threatened her. He couldn't accept Parul's physical transformation. She, on the other hand, is no longer afraid of him.

A saline drip is being given to Parul. She's about to pass away. She has already received three bags of blood intravenously. Bhavani is waiting outside. The expression on her face conveys a sense of apprehension.

Parul's body budges a little bit. She's regaining consciousness. Her hand fumbles around the bed, looking for something. Bhavani walks and gently rests her loving hand on Parul's head. Parul slowly opens her eyes. At the same time, the Nurse enters the room. The lovely wail of a newborn infant fills the air.

****

2

Cancer

Tarik Anowar

The bell has sounded to signal the end of the classes. Sukanta glances at his wristwatch. 'You have not been taught anything new today,' he replies, looking at the students. The school time is over now. Sukanta has been appointed as a Math teacher at this school, but because he belongs to the Scheduled Caste, he is not permitted to teach the subject. To put it another way, he is recruited in the lower caste reserved group. They believe he lacks a solid understanding of Maths. As a result, if he teaches Math to kids, they will not understand it properly. That's why he is not allowed to teach Math.

He's been instructed to exclusively take Work Education classes. In this school, Sukanto is the lone Scheduled Caste teacher. As a result, he had no one to speak for him.

He has had no choice but to accept this decision. In addition, he has been denied access to the Teaching Staff Room. He's even told to drink from the tube-well outside, where the students get their water. Sukanta was a Ramakrishna Mission student in Purulia. He is a polite and modest man. He has acclimated to such a prejudiced environment and hopes that one day he would be able to claim the dignity of his identity.

It's sweltering outside. It's as if the sun had poured all of its energy onto the planet. Sukanta uses his handkerchief to wipe away the sweat. Standing in front of a store, he drinks a glass of lemon water. Sukanta moves forward after paying the money when he is stopped by a familiar voice from behind.... 'Sukanta, Sukanto, please wait....'

'Tithi, you are here?' He can't believe his eyes.

Tithi approaches Sukanto at that point, saying, 'You're surprised, aren't you?'

'Yes, that's all.'

'Sukanta, please explain me why you came to Kolkata without informing me? You haven't even given us any information?'

'It's all right; I didn't want to get you in trouble since your mother was upset.' Now, tell me, Tithi, why are you here, in Kolkata?'

'I've been teaching for a few months at a college.'

'In which college do you teach?'

'Vidyasagar College.'

'Where did you intend to go this way?'

'Actually, I was planning on doing some shopping in Garia Haat Market.'

'All right, then, let's go in that direction.'

'All right, let's go.'

A silence had descended between them. Tithi vividly recalls that day.

'Sukanta, why do you always act so irrationally? What happened to you?'

'That's nothing.'

'What do you mean by nothing? I am quite certain that something has gone wrong with you. Can you tell me what happened?'

'Please just go away; you are bugging me. Please leave me alone.'

'Sukanta, is there any matter of discontent between you and Priyanka? If you tell me, I can act as a mediator to help you resolve it.'

'Whoops! Why would she be the source of any dissatisfaction?'

'I've noticed that you haven't spoken to her in a few days.'

'I don't think it's worth my time to talk to her.'

Tithi is aware that they were in love. But then something had awful happened, and their relationship was shattered. They've been in a genuine relationship since they were children. Tithi noticed Priyanka strolling alongside Palash a few days ago. Tithi is upset when she sees Sukanta's pallid face. Tithi has no idea why this is the case. Is she then in love with Sukanta?

Sukanta, Palash, Sakti, Tamal, Priyanka, and Tithi are all students at the same university. They are also excellent buddies. They are all free to visit one other's homes. Nilima Devi, Tithi's mother, has a soft corner for Sukanta. She contacts him at home whenever a need arises. Can anyone resist falling in love with a boy who always has a smile on his face?

'Aunty, don't give it to me anymore; I can't eat it all.' Sukanta uses his hand to cover his plate. 'Aunty, give him a little more; he likes to eat hotchpotch,' Palash replies as he removes Sukanta's hand. Sukanta is self-conscious. Nilima Devi adds two more spoons to his plate.

'My mother has called you, Sukanta.'

'What for, Tithi?'

'Once you get here, you'll find out.'

'Is there anything special?'

'Perhaps.'

'Then I have to leave.'

'Sukanta, do you want me to tell you something?'

'Yes, please tell me.'

'Actually, no...'

'Say anything you want. What's the matter with you?'

'Not today,' she says.

'Why won't you say, Tithi, tell me now? Anything should not be suppressed.'

Tithi is unable to say it once more. How would she show Sukanta how much shc adores him?

'Will you not tell me?' Sukanta says again.

'Not now,' Tithi answers softly, staring at the ground. 'I'll tell you later.'

Sukanta looks at Tithi in amazement. He doesn't say anything. 'Sukanta, will you be able to come to our house tomorrow afternoon?'

'What's the matter, Aunty?'

'Tithi and I are going shopping together. It would be nice if you could join us. Actually, my child and I can count on you.'

'All right, Aunty, I'll go.'

'Sukanta, eat with us before you leave.'

'No, Aunty, not today, but on some other day.'

Sukanta pays Tithi's house a visit every now and then. Nilima Aunty adores him as if he were a son, and it is impossible for him to ignore her love and affection. She cares for him as if he were her own child.

'Sukanta, I've made *Naru* especially for you because you enjoy it so much.'

'Yes, *Naru* is my favourite. My mother, too, cooks *Naru* in a delectable way.'

'Is that it?' But I'm afraid I won't be able to prepare it so well. Taste it, how it is?' she says, removing the jar's cover.

'It's delicious' – he responds by biting a piece of *Naru.*

'Are you serious, Sukanta?'

'Yes, Aunty, it is pretty tasty.'

Sukanta holds Nilima Devi in high regard. Their house's door is always open for him. Tithi's mother has a different opinion about Sukanta among all his friends. Her feelings for him are always stronger than those for others.

Sukanta was completely unaware of this when he fell in love with Tithi. Tithi's eyes welled up with tears of joy the first time Sukanta told her about his love. They reached a point in their relationship where they wanted to marry and commit to each other for the rest of their lives. Because Tithi is an upper caste lady and Sukanta is from the Namashudra caste, all the trouble and frustration begin here. This marriage is doomed to fail. Kind-hearted Sukanta feels irritation in his eyes.

'Listen Tithi. This marriage is unacceptable to me. I will never allow a Namashudra to be your groom.'

'But, Mom, isn't he also very much loved by you?'

'I adored him,' she said. 'I liked him since he looked to be a really courteous boy and a good friend of yours, but I can't accept him as a son-in-law. We'll arrange for your marriage to take place in a civilised family somewhere else. Have you forgotten who we are as *Kulin Brahmins*?'

Palash appeared unexpectedly at Tithi's house one morning. As soon as the calling bell rang, Nilima Devi opened the door. 'What's the issue, Palash, why are you here so early in the morning?'

'Aunty, where is Tithi?' 'Go, she is in that room,' Nilima Devi replies pointing her finger at the corner room.

'May I come in?'

Looking at the door Tithi answers – 'yes come in.'

'Oho! What has caused your health to decline so drastically? How did you get so skinny?'

'Palash, I'm not in the best of health.'

'However, your mother is exaggerating. She had the option of accepting it.'

'No, it will never, ever happen. I am quite familiar with my mum.'

'Tithi, Sukanta has a job and has relocated to Kolkata. He resigned from his job here.'

'Do you have any idea where he went?'

'No, I'm not sure.' He didn't provide me with an address. However, he informed me that he had enrolled in a school in Baliganj.'

'How is he doing these days?'

'He, too, is ill.' He inquired about you, but I was unable to provide any information. In fact, it's been a long time since I've spoken with you.'

'Tithi, did you hear Tamal got a job offer in Bangalore? He's relocated to that location. I'm also about to look for jobs; it's in the process, and I'm looking forward to starting within the next month.'

'How's Priyanka? How's she doing?'

'She is quite talented. Let me break the good news to you: I'm getting married to Priyanka in a month. You must show up for the wedding ceremony.'

'I'll do my best.' But I can't say for certain.'

'However, we hope you will come.'

Nilima Devi, Tithi's mother, appears to have gone utterly silent. She doesn't say anything for the entire day. Tithi is no longer interested in anything. In the meantime, her uncle presents her with a marriage proposal. That was, of course, their sister's strict command. Tithi, despite her fatigued body, is forced to sit in a chair and dress up like a bride. She's annoyed because she's been bombarded with questions. Tithi thinks about her father a lot because she feels helpless. This incident would not have occurred if her father had been alive. She attempts to picture her father's face in her mind's eye. But she can't recall anything other than a foggy appearance in her thoughts. Her throat appears to make a weeping sound. '*Baba....*' comes out of her throat in an unclear voice.

The doorbell rings unexpectedly. 'Tithi, take a look at who's arrived.' A peon delivers her a note as soon as she opens the door. Tithi says, 'Ma, I have gotten a job,' after glancing at the letter.

'Job?'

'Yes, Ma, here is the letter'

'Tell me where it is, let me see.' She begins to read the letter she is holding. 'You've been offered a position at Calcutta College.'

'Yes, Ma, I have to report on June 2nd.'

'How are you going to accomplish the job in Kolkata by yourself?'

'Why, Ma, there are a lot of girls who are working.'

'Where will you stay?'

'Why.... in a hostel.'

Tithi relocates to Kolkata for work almost against her mother's wishes.

'Perhaps reuniting with you isn't auspicious, Tithi.'

'Why, if we didn't love each other, would things be different?'

'I have no knowledge about it, but if Aunty finds out, she will chastise you.'

'Look, Sukanta, I've matured into a young woman; I know what's best for me.'

Sukanta remains silent, only taking a deep, lengthy breath that pierces his chest.

But, in the end, Tithi must confess her defeat to her mother. Because the truth cannot be concealed forever. One day or the other, truth is to be revealed. As a result, the news of their reunion of hearts reached her mother in Durgapur. Tithi's mother realises that it would be inappropriate if her daughter elopes and gets engaged with him. That's why, she consents to their marriage. She invites Sukanta's parents to her house one day. They converse with one another. Sukanta's parents were ready to give their consent to the marriage from the very beginning, just after looking his face. They have given their consent with tremendous joy even today.

On the wedding night, Sukanta places a ring on Tithi's finger. He believes they are all worthless because they are marrying out of love. Tithi, on the other hand, has a different perspective on the situation. Her rage is well restrained. After all, the jewellery Sukanta's relatives had given her did not match her preferences. She is completely dissatisfied for all of these reasons. She verbally criticises Sukanta, bringing up his caste, and smashes household items in a fit of wrath all day. Sukanta is then subjected to physical and emotional abuse. He escaped to a friend's house after leaving his room. Tithi was furious and headed to her parents' house. Her mother, Nilima Devi, has stated unequivocally that they will not accept any responsibility because she chose to marry a lower caste man. As a result, Tithi has no choice but to return to her father-in-law's residence. She is able to contain her rage now. Her pride in her caste identity, though, is still agitated. She disdains her spouse now and then, alluding to his low-caste status. Sukanta is in a bad mood today. With his eyes closed, he is lying on his bed in his room. He has no idea when the evening has turned into the night. He didn't switch on the light in the room because it didn't provide any hope. He was unable to tell anyone about what had occurred at school today. He has been compelled to take Work Education classes despite the fact that he is a Math teacher, and he has quietly tolerated it in the hope that one day he will be treated with dignity. But how will he deal with what happened today? Tears welled up in his eyes. Every single cell in his body trembles. Sukanta unlocked the school gate and proceeded to the office room, where the attendance record was kept to be signed, as he had done the day before. Suddenly, some individuals approached him from behind and began striking him with sticks on the head and back. When he turned around, he found that all of his students who had participated in his P.T. session the day before had leapt on him for beating. 'Hit the idiot, the queer, and take him out of the school,' someone says from afar. Sukanta, half-dead and humiliated, keeps asking, 'What are you doing?' like a madman. 'What is the reason for doing this? You can't act like that around me?' He had, however, already been pushed out of the gate by that time. The suddenness of the incident left him bewildered and astonished. Sukanta travelled home while dragging his worn-out body in his wake. He was trying to fall asleep while lying in bed, but he was having trouble. It seems that the embarrassing incident from earlier in the day was slowly killing him. He wonders whether there isn't a way to undo such wrongdoings. Will we always be the targets of such scepticism and hostility? Sukanta's bodily fatigue is abruptly lifted. He is unsure of the cause of his clenched fists. He feels as though his jaw is being restricted.

****

3

The Conflict

Saddam Saikh

The darkness of the sky which is seen through an open window and on the light-post where it stands still appears to be close, but Banani knows that it is a long way away. She had been resting on the bed for a long time with her eyes closed. Tears were streaming down the side of the loaded eyes, but no one noticed. The darkness is pitch black and dense. The silence of darkness has a dreadful beauty to it. And that horrible, dreadful beauty is looking for a home in Banani's head. It's almost two o'clock at night. On the street, there is no sound of human footsteps. The tung-tang sound of rickshaws occasionally breaks the night's silence. Banani gets out of bed and walks down the hall. Tumpa is sleeping soundly in her bed. Banani walks up to the sink and washes her face and eyes. Then she goes to the window and stands there. For the past three days, Kalyan has been sleeping in his mother's room. Banani is baffled as to why he behaves in this manner at times. They married because they loved each other. Renuka Kanjilal, Kalyan's mother, is a high school teacher. Her only kid is Kalyan. She lost her husband when she was young and raised her kid alone, eventually rising to the position she holds now despite adversity. Kalyan is now a well-known physician.

'I am a girl from Colony Para, I acquainted with Kalyan in a music school. He was a Medical College student at the time. Then one day, that conversation evolved into love. He would take me to the banks of the Ganges. We'd walk a long distance together. On the other hand, the sun would suddenly vanish after scattering some *Abir* across the sky. There were two or four stars in the sky. And under that open sky we could see its incredible blooming. Banani Mandal, the daughter of the Colony Para, was no longer my identity. I used to forget that I would have to go to the line of Tubewell for water after going back from here. Instead, I began to think that I reached the stairs of heaven. As a result, I became estranged from my previous existence. My mind started to work in a unique way.

To put it another way, Akash got into my head quite a bit. When I used to go to the library with him, I would walk along the road under the Spanish cherry tree instead of going straight to the library. On the way, Kalyan would pick one or two flowers and give them to me. If there was a moon in the sky, the shadow of the tree and the road that passed through its gap appeared to be on the other side of the earth. Do you recall Sapna that day when you reminded me and tried to warn me? I chuckled at your statements that day. That day, I didn't understand and didn't even try to understand. I'd never considered it in that light before. It never occurred to me that human beings could be divided. I used to imagine a time when casteism existed, and how that casteism would infect the human mind in a society that is now flourishing with enlightenment. Kalyan is a doctor and a public servant. That's why it didn't even cross my thoughts. Do you remember that afternoon Sapna, it was my birthday, and he came to our house for the first time?'

'Please sing a song, Kalyan *Da*? Let's start the birthday cake with your song in this function.' While handing over the harmonium to Kalyan, Sapna again said that – 'man's voice should be powerful and melodious. It would be like the flood breaking the coast and the danger overwhelming the area. There should be no time for the audience to catch their breath.' Kalyan took the harmonium with a warm smile … Then he sang:

> 'All that my heart desires for
> You are the one that you are.'

'My colony's houses were cluttered. The gap was only a few inches. As a result, the secret would be out. The majority of the residents in the area ran a small business or worked at a printing press, and a few were employed by the government. Some people came to listen to Kalyan's song. The singing session did not come to a halt till the wee hours of the morning.'

Banani's elbow is grasped by Kalyan. It was the end of the day. That was the point at which the world began to become thick. Banani stepped nearer, his eyes twinkling. They forged onward, breaking the sand path. 'Let's travel to the Sundarbans,' Kalyan suggests, before the silence fades. 'Banani, after we arrive, we'll attend the launch; it'll be a lot of fun, won't it?'

Banani is deafeningly quiet. Kalyan's hand is tighter around her index finger. 'I wanted to say softly that I will go everywhere with the one I love and the one who loves me,' he continues. 'But…..'

'But, what Banani?'

Banani remains silent.

'Oh, I realise that if I wish to touch the girl who is walking alongside me, I need an infinite staircase. Ok Banani, so be it next month.' Kalyan burst out laughing at his own remarks. Banani joined in the giggling.

Banani was sitting with the harmonium this morning, hardly able to play the music when a raspy voice pierced her eardrums. 'Do you understand, you low caste girl, that there would be no song or music here? It is not customary in the Kanjilal dynasty for the housewives to shout at the top of their voice. You must be courteous here.' Renuka Devi, Banani's mother-in-law, climbed up the steps while pressing her foot after saying the words. Banani stands up quickly and looks back as Kalyan places his hand on her shoulder. To lighten the mood and make things a little easier, he asked, 'Do you still want to learn music? However, if mother does not want you to learn the song, you should refrain from singing or caring for it. You have to give up Banani. You do not need to study; you don't have to do M.A.' Then the tone of the Kalyan's voice softens a little – 'Banani, you have studied a lot, and now please focuses on your family as much as possible; you don't need to work.'

Banani is rooted to the spot. She cannot imagine – Is the same Kalyan or someone else?

'But how is this possible Kalyan? Song has been a part of my thoughts and body since I was a toddler. I don't know how I'm going to let it go. Isn't it true that my music captivated you? My father wasn't a particularly good vocalist, but he was an avid listener. He used to take tunes and write songs in between jobs. I began learning from my father when I was a child. In Colony Para, my mother used to cook late on many nights, and Dad would then close his eyes and try tunes fervently. My mum forbade me from working. I recall quite a bit from when I was in high school. There was a lot of pressure on me to finish my education. She would sit next to me and read until I fell asleep. Mother was in a bad mood. Maybe that's how she tried to confine her universe where we have no legal right to be in that world One day, I hurried to my father because he was crying, and I realised my mother was out of breath, and Dad was trying to blow fresh air into her brain. Everything came to an end with my father's scream while I was fetching the water in the bucket. I couldn't stop my father. He too walked away from the world after defeating his attachment to her.'

'Sapna, there are countless black spots all over my body. These represent my husband's and mother-in-law's love for me. I could not listen to their words. I couldn't quit singing. They beat me. Kalyan is no longer the same Kalyan as before. He goes to the height of cruelty because of my terrified expression. If I hadn't become acquainted with the present Kalyan, I would have been unaware that people could be so cruel. I have a little girl named Tumpa. I desperately want to keep Tumpa with you. You don't have any children. I can't think of anyone else right now except you. I'm scared to death. Day and night appear to me to be a nightmare. Make Tumpa a doctor, but one who is more well-known than her father…'

'Your desire has been fulfilled, mother, I have become a doctor today', Tumpa said inaudibly. She cherishes her mother's diary, which she keeps on her chest. Tumpa discovered her mother's diary among old books this morning. Tumpa has trouble remembering her mother's face; a hazy shadow floats in front of her eyes. In her mind's eye, a dim image appears. There are a lot of people in the house, yet everyone is quite calm. Mother has been laid on the bed in the yard outside. Near the head, incense sticks are burning. Mother has a dark ebony complexion. She cries as she stares at the terrible face. Perhaps she is frightened. Someone carries her away in his lap, possibly to a distant location. Tumpa learns that her mother's stove had caught fire and that she was burned. She couldn't be taken to the hospital after that. It was all over before that. Tumpa's head began to tingle, and her eyes began to water unconsciously. It was as if everything had sprung to life in front of her eyes. Tumpa let out a piercing scream, 'no no…. this cannot happen…. never ever…'

****

4

The Paw

Tarik Anowar

'You know, *Boudi*. We have to leave Dumdum after ten or twelve years.'

Barnali is taken aback and asks Shiuli, 'Why are you talking like this?'

'One day, my father and uncles were talking how we can no longer afford to stay here at the current pace of increase in our house rent. We must go with all of our possessions towards the village. But *Boudi*, I don't want to leave this spot at all,' Shiuli says again as she pours water into the pot.

'It doesn't matter. You'll be living here. From here, your daughter will learn.'

'No, *Boudi*, I'm thinking of something else right now.' Where will we go with so many people if the landlord of the house passes over the land to the promoter? All our homes will be demolished. Perhaps a massive apartment will be built here. So, *Boudi*, where else are we going?'

It's as though I've forgotten what the solution is. 'There is no point in thinking about that,' I respond with a smile on my face.

'It's better if it's not.' Shiuli speaks in hushed tones.

'Aunty, will you not prepare tea?' Tina asks turning over the pages of the book that was kept on the table.

'Of course! Start making the tea, Shiuli. Your daughter is looking forward to having tea.'

Tina is Shiuli's five-year-old daughter. She attends a school that teaches English as a second language. When she comes to see us, she only brings books with her. Because of her wit, she draws everyone's attention. Shiuli is illiterate as well. She has completed class nine of her education.

Even just a few years ago, unoccupied land could be purchased. However, there is currently no vacant land available in this area. Houses have been built all over the place. The colossal flats are so large that they seem to touch the sky. After removing the old houses, new towering buildings are being built.

'Sukla *Di*, haven't you been living here for quite some time?'

'Yes, Bornali, my grandpa came to this country from East Pakistan. The *Chanrals*, on the other hand, were on the verge of capturing this region. *Chanral Para* was the name given to this location in the past. This is where they used to grow paddy.'

'Shukla *Di*, what happened to them?' Bornali is taken aback.

'They sold the lands for a good price, and then they migrated to the villages.' They buy cheap agricultural lands and cultivate paddy there. In the metropolis, they have nothing to do.'

'That is correct.'

Bornali's mind wanders to another thought. When their lands are overflowing with grain, the city's ravenous wolves will return to drain their blood. As a result, they will be compelled to relocate once more. Then somewhere else.....

Every day, the three women – Bornali, Sukla, and Keka go for a morning walk together. After a morning walk, they all gathered at Bornali's house today.

'However, Bornali, everyone has not left this place.'

Sukla *Di's* booming voice jolts Bornali out of her reverie and back into the conversation. 'There are still some *Chanral* family who live here.' However, they are few in number. By educating themselves, some of them look to be *Bhadralok*.'

'Sukla *Di*, black will take no other hue. *Chanral's* blood cannot be washed away by putting on a gentlemen's mask.' This is said ironically by Keka *Di*.

'What exactly are you talking about, Keka *Di*?' Talking about individuals with such disrespect...'

Bornali's words were still incomplete.

'They are born with the *Sonar Chamooch* [Golden Spoon] in their mouth. Every employment sector has reserved seats for them.'

'You have the incorrect idea. That's only 15%, and even that quota isn't distributed fairly.'

'Don't talk rubbish; our children are not getting good opportunities because of them, even though they have high grades. Consider the farmers of Singur, who are plotting against the government's plan. The government is acquiring land for the construction of industries, but they are opposing. Farmers are unwilling to give up their land. Only when industries are formed can the country's unemployment crisis be alleviated. A sigh of relief will be heard from the educated youths. How will these farmers realise its importance? Had they known the value of letters, they would have realised its significance.'

Bornali stays out of any further debate. The morning walk's soothing effect has worn off on her today. Keka *Di's* remarks continue to reverberate in her head.

The acquisition of rural farmers' land is required for large-scale industrialisation and urbanisation. What about rural development? Villages are still isolated and difficult to reach. There are no excellent roads or sources of safe drinking water in the area. The poor residents of the villages are frequently afflicted by food shortages. The electric poles have been erected solely for the purpose of displaying them without the use of electricity. Electricity is only available for a few hours a day. Villagers who are poor are denied a variety of opportunities. The majority of the villagers are uneducated and farmers by profession, with a large proportion of farmers owning no land. They toil as slaves in other people's agricultural lands. Only if landlords graciously allow them to cultivate their lands, they can harvest paddy. They can only manage a handful of rice despite putting forth a lot of effort. Landowners will benefit if they sell these agricultural lands to industrialists at a high price, but poor peasants and sharecroppers would starve to death. They won't be able to cultivate any land. In the age of high-tech liberalisation, what types of jobs will be available to illiterate farmers? Farmers in Nandigram continue to demonstrate in order to keep their ancestral lands. They are unwilling to relinquish their lands to industrialisation since it will not improve their livelihoods. They have been cultivating and reaping gold in their territories, and they intend to continue doing so. However, due to the government's tremendous pressure, their desire would be fully destroyed one day. If one approaches them, one can hear their crying sounds. Bornali turns off the television.

Was Shiuli then correct? *Chanral* Caste is the owner of the house in which she rents. The house has a number of modest rooms that are completely desolate. The politically motivated promoters' aggressive hand will one day seize that house in the name of a phoney pretext, and the destitute lower caste people like Shiuli will once again be refugees. Poor farmers will lose their fields and houses as a result of opportunistic, wealthy traders putting their paws in this way with governmental intervention.

****

5

Shelter

Saddam Saikh

Manab *Babu* is out of sorts today. He is down with a slight fever. The doctor arrived in the later hours of the day. The doctor cautioned against catching a cold. He feels exhausted if he does not go for a brief walk in the afternoon. He's not in the mood to come downstairs today. He is standing on the second-floor balcony, looking up at the distant sky. The sun is now setting. The sun's crimson has tinted the western horizon.

'Dad…'

'Who, Paromita?'

'Yes, dad. I was stuck in a terrible traffic jam; that being the case I have been late to get home. The driver did not show up today. I've come by myself.'

'You shouldn't have driven such a long distance. You've taken too many risks.'

'O my God, your body is burning with a high temperature,' she exclaims as she steps towards the door, holding father's hand. 'I'm not going to listen to you today. You must accompany me to the doctor.'

'It isn't necessary. I'm having a good time here. Here, I'm treated well. In the morning, Doctor *Babu* came to see me and gave me medicine. There are individuals here who will look after me. Do not be concerned about me.'

The night is approaching. Tears well up in the eyes of Paromita. She ascends the second-floor stairwell. This 'Old Age Home' is built on several acres of land. When someone walks through the gate, they will be greeted by a large signboard. 'Old Age Home' is written in big letters. The path leads right to the front of the massive four-story home after passing through the gate. On both sides of the road, there are flower beds. The fir and salt cedar trees line the length of the yard. Paromita looks back once. Her father's unwavering stare remains riveted on her.

At the youthful age of 16, Alka came here as a daughter-in-law. Then, in pride and arrogance, a long period of time passes. Frequent calls are coming from the nursing home. Alka's son and daughter inquire about her. 'How's it going, mom?' 'Hello, my name is Shipra, and I am Alka Devi's daughter.'

He is still unconscious and is being flushed with saline. We can't say anything till we've waited 48 hours. The entire house is crammed to the brim with people. The jewels are wrapped in a red sari and placed on the cot over there in the corner. Near his head, incense is burning. Tuberoses are used to embellish the crib. People who are close to the body are in grief. The grandmother is surrounded by a gaggle of grandchildren. Tears are welling up in their eyes. It appears as if a few people are dying at Alka's feet. They'll snap a photograph of Alka's footprint on the paper and save it as a memento. Married women wish their husbands by rubbing vermillion on their foreheads and scalps. Manab *Babu* has cried aloud and dried his eyes. He approaches Alka's head and takes a position close to it. The woman whom you have known for a long time is embarking on an eternal journey. Her hands are clasped together over her chest. With these hands extended out, she will never come to ask for anything. 'I've had so much sleep! Are you sleeping, Alka? But I don't have that sleepy look in my eyes any longer. Alka...Alka...' his heart is breaking with an intense suppressed heart-rending cry. With both hands, Manab *Babu* cups his face.

'Will you accompany me to the crematorium, Dad?'

'Yes, I will,'

The car has arrived. When everyone has gathered, the car will depart for the Crematorium…

'Why younger sisters are being late to turn up?'

'Promise me Alka that you will stand by my side till your last breath.'

'Hey, I'm staying with you. Where will I go leaving you? I will be by your side for the rest of my life' – Alka murmured, her face hidden in Manab *Babu's* chest. 'However, today that Alka...' the eyelids begin to droop. Today, the weary body appears to be a burden. Priya is sobbing uncontrollably and slamming his head into his father's chest. Priya is Manab *Babu's* youngest daughter. Dad is completely silent. He only tenderly touches Priya's forehead with his fingers at irregular intervals.

'What is the reason for my younger sisters' delay in arriving?' – Manab *Babu's* youngest kid, Akash, snaps out. 'Priya, have your tea'. By the time Priya had composed herself. The second *Pishima* comes holding a tea tray in her hands. Taking the cup off her *Pishima's* hand, Priya tells her 'keep the keys of mom's Almirah carefully, we will go to the crematorium early in the morning and one more thing I have forgotten to ask you – have you made the arrangement for lunch?'

Priti and Shipra have arrived long ago. They have made all the arrangements. Pulse and steamed rice are cooked.

'Make sure the kids are fed on time. Your son-in-law can't bear hunger.'

Hungry Paromita is walking around with dry face. She is Alka's third daughter. She has arrived a short while ago. Her spouse and son have not accompanied her. Paromita sat close to her mother's head, staring at her for a long time. Mom will never open her eyes again. She will never call me by my name Paromita. Paromita bawls uncontrollably.

The eldest daughter is putting the jewels away after opening the Almirah with the key. Dad gave her a distant look but said nothing. Otunu, the oldest son, and Biddut, the middle son, have been arguing for a long time. He gave them a single glance before standing outside, as if he wanted to be alone for a moment. A spell of uncontrollable wailing of mourning people tears apart the entire house together with the echo of the words *Bolohori...Horibol...* Manab *Babu's* chest echoes with the tune of eternal farewell. Alka looked stunning in a crimson sari. The Dom wanted to remove her sari before transporting her to the furnace. That was not allowed by Manab *Babu.* Alka's favourite sari was that one. She used to look stunning picking flowers with a flower basket in her hand while wearing this sari. Today, Alka will be burned to ashes.

'This is my mother's bone, *Babu.* Float it down the Ganga'. He immediately spreads his palm and grabs it, the last evidence of Alka. He caresses it with great fondness.

'Dad, let's go; we've got to get back.'

Funeral activities are still ongoing. As if it were a festival home, the house is still crammed with people. Manab *Babu* is looking out the open window of the room.

'Dad, we wanted to say something to you.' The older and younger sons go into the room together.

'Dad, we ask that you divide the mother's possessions amongst us so that we can advance in the business.'

'Are you of the same mind, my middle son?'

'Yes dad. Dad, we were also thinking about you. What will you do if you're alone in this old house? That is why we have decided that you will alternate staying at our homes for some days.' Shipra, the eldest daughter, arrived by that time. 'We have an equal share in the property,' Shipra says quickly. Dad raises his eyes to her. Shipra's face is flushed.

'My sister-in-law, *Dada Babu*, has given birth to a baby daughter.' – Haru delivers the breaking news in a hurried manner. He's been at home for quite some time.

'What are you doing standing there?' Take two cruses full of sweets with you. Alka, your daughter looks like you.'

Leaving the realms of thought and meditation Manab *Babu* expresses his wish for a peaceful funeral process, stating that the home is overflowing with guests. The eldest son Otunu and the youngest son Biddut are dragging their feet out of the house. Shipra, on the other hand, remains motionless.

'Should I bring you a cup of tea, Dad?' Manab *Babu* is deafeningly quiet. He glances out the window silently. The patio is sweltering with heat. Paromita is simply strolling through the house. Mother's memories are reflected all over the place. The stench of mothers' bodies may still be detected in the air. She inhales deeply, smelling the odour to her heart's pleasure. As if dad has become dumb. As if his age has been increased by ten years in these few days. Paromita can't look at the face of the lonely man.

'Go with me.'

'Where?'

'To my house. You no longer have reasons to stay here. I will leave tomorrow morning. Be prepared.'

That was the departure of Manab *Babu*. Dad did not go with Paromita. He came on his own to this old age home. He bequeathed all of his property to his sons and daughters before being relocated here, with the exception of a little portion set aside for himself. He came to this old age home all alone without informing others. After a lot of searching, Paromita found her father in this old age home. That's also after five years later. That day she discovered a folded paper in her father's room. She dashed out of the house with the letter in her hand.

Manab *Babu's* youngest son has recently got married. After fixing the date of marriage, he came to take his father with him but dad did not go. Rather his father told 'I bless you from here, be happy.' The son brought his wife over to meet her father-in-law one day. The eldest and middle sons did not even show up for a single visit. They have a lot of work ahead of them. They are too preoccupied with their business to come around here and look for their father. As if the pastdays seem very odd to Manab *Babu.* He has an excruciating discomfort in his chest. He takes a stride towards the house, both hands on his chest.

****

6

Brain Wash

Tarik Anowar

It is almost eleven or half past eleven at night when Saro returns home after work. Her husband comes out of the room on the street and starts walking hither and thither on the road anxiously. Then he breathes a sigh of relief to see her arrival. Saro lives with her husband, son and daughter at a slum in Dumdum in a small room of 10 X 10 feet and a porch attached to it. She dwells in a destitute condition with her family. There is not even a single window in the room for ventilation. Three members somehow settle themselves in such a small abode. Her children study in that packed room and go to school. Her husband Bablu Mondal is a retail vegetable seller. But he is a lethargic to some extent; if he goes to work one day, then he escapes next three days. The price of goods in the market is skyrocketing now. His business is not going well expectedly. Saro somehow pays the rent of the room working as a maid in other's houses. Moreover, the electric bill, her children's tuition fees and medical expenses etc. depend on that income. Often her husband says in a pleading manner – 'Saro, stop the son's education. I can't afford the family alone anymore, better you set him working somewhere. Then the family will recover a little from its scarcity.'

'Why? Do you pay for his education?' Saro replies sharply. She controls herself and says in a humble tone – 'I will not let him stop studying. I want him to study more.' Saro herself studied till class six. She can only read books and sign her name. But Bablu never crossed the threshold of the school. He did not get the opportunity to be with the man of letters. He was a kind of blind man towards education though he had eyes.

'Saro, I didn't study, so what happened? Am I not making money by doing business? It is a luxury to study in a miserable family like ours.'

'No matter what you tell me or what you try to explain, I will not let my children stop studying as long as I am alive. No matter how hard it gets, I will do everything possible to bring them up with good education.'

Saro recalls her childhood days. Her mother was beaten by her father as she admitted Saro to the school without her father's consent. Yet she did not stop sending her to school. But in the end, she had to accept the defeat as her father compelled her to marry Bablu. At that time Saro was in class six.

The road seems to be crowdless today and a chill on the way. Saro feels little scared to walk all alone. A while ago, it rained cats and dogs. The blowing breeze seems cold enough. It's about half past eleven at night. It was a little late in cooking as some guests have come to the Mess today. Her body looks very tired and exhausted. Saro doesn't seem to have time to rest these days. She has to go out to work in the very early morning. Once she returns home at noon and then again, she has to go out to work in the afternoon. It is almost half past ten or eleven o'clock when she returns home. Her son Tapos has given final exam in the school and Minu, her daughter is studying in class nine. She has to bear the expense of a handsome amount of money for their education. Saro has to face a lot of difficulties to manage everything alone.

Now, it has almost been a year since Bablu left them behind. One-night Bablu suddenly fell ill. He breathed his last on the way to the hospital. Today Saro is completely alone. When Saro used to return home with her fatigued body, Bablu became busy and said – 'Saro, you take off your clothes, I'm fetching water from the well and then wash your body. You return home so late night; I'm worried about you.'

'Why are you worried? Am I a little girl?'

'You will not understand, had you been a man you would have realised it.'

Saro is really scared today. He carelessly left the world leaving all the responsibilities of the family on her shoulders. He had a desire to live long. That day when Bablu was fighting with Death in the house, he tightly clasped Saro's hand. Her eyes were almost dried out. It was as if her chest trembled at an unknown fear. How soon would they try to reach the hospital? But all of a sudden, his hand fists were loosened, and the movement of his body was stopped. The people around Saro were startled by her screams. A deep sigh pierced out of her chest. A few days ago, the final examination result of the son had been released in the school. He had passed the examination. Now he needs a large amount of money to be admitted in the new class. Where from will she manage that amount of money? Two months later she will have to organise her husband's annual mourning ceremony. Moreover, the Brahmin priest commanded – there is some disorder in her husband's horoscope. In order to avoid that mishap, they need to organise a sacrificial (Yaggo) ceremony. Otherwise, three members of the family will die. To perform the sacrificial ceremony, they need four thousand rupees. From where will she manage this amount and who will give her that money? They may accumulate some amount by selling the old sew-machine of their house. One day, she told Roma *Boudi*, whose house she worked in, about the sacrificial ceremony. She laughed hearing about it and said – 'Saro, there is nothing left after the death of a human being. Finding disorders in the horoscope is a kind of trick of the Brahmin priest for earning money. Now you should think about the admission of your son.' But the advice of Roma *Boudi* seems unacceptable to her. She keeps muttering in herself – 'no, there must be some defect otherwise how the mishappening took place. Let people say whatever, everything happened because of the fault in horoscope. The boy could have suffered more. No, no, there should not be delay anymore; we have to complete the sacrificial ceremony as soon as possible.'

'Saro, what are you thinking since long? You have not washed the utensils yet.'

'Yes *Boudi*, I am going to wash.' Promptly, she starts washing the utensils. She seems to be startled a little. Roma *Boudi* observes her carefully.

'Saro, have you brought your son's admission form? If it is too late, the forms will not be available anymore.'

'No *Boudi*, not yet.'

'You have not brought it yet? Did I not tell you to bring the form taking leave of one day from your work?'

'No *Boudi*, I think not to admit him this year.'

'Why?'

'*Boudi*, he has passed this year. And I am planning to continue his education from next year.'

'Saro, it will hamper his educational pace, he will lag behind one year.'

'What to do, *Boudi*? I have to arrange the sacrificial ceremony to remove the disorder of their father's horoscope.'

****

7

Quicksand

Saddam Saikh

Mukulesh takes the last train back home. He was stuck in an urgent work. The piercing cold appears to be vibrating through the sweater and into the body. Taking the shawl out of the bag he swaddles it around his body. Tranquility is prevailing in the street. A few people disembark from the train and proceed to various streets. All the street lamps are not lit up. As a result, it appears darker. He lights a cigarette, his lone buddy in this world of solitude. It is not too far. The house is a few steps ahead of the turning of the pond.

What is that, what is fallen there? Mukulesh moves forward. What is this! This is a new born baby. What brings him here? There is also a milk bottle by his side. Who has abandoned him here? He has closed his eyes. Mukulesh approaches the baby and places his hand on the baby's chest. The baby is still alive, but he is dosing off. Mukulesh then takes a rapid step towards his house.

As soon as he enters the gate of the house, he yells out – 'Mala, O… Mala, open the door quickly.'

'What's going on, and why are you screaming?' – Mala inquires as she opens the door.

'Take a look at who I've brought.'

'Whom?' She is taken aback as she opens the door. Whom have you brought?

'He was abandoned near Tumpa's house, wrapped in a cloth.'

'Please hand over the infant to me.'

Mala takes the infant from Mukulesh's lap and says, 'Oh, he's gone asleep.' Then she wonders aloud, 'Who has left such a small breastfeeding infant here; is he completely devoid of human kindness?' News gets around in the village in the wee hours of the next day morning. People come to see in groups. The morning passes away responding to people's questions, and the midday hour arrives. Mala has just finished bathing the baby and is getting ready to dress him.

'What's the matter, Mala *Boudi*; it's been overheard that you've brought a stranded infant home.' Shefali arrives and takes a position at the door.

'Yes.'

'Can you tell me where you discovered the baby?'

'I did not discover the infant. Your elder brother discovered.'

'Where was the baby stranded?'

'Your elder brother has informed that the baby was stranded near the house of Tumpa.'

'Oh! It is so. Then, surely it is Tumpa's activity.'

'Shefali, nothing can be said based on a conjecture.'

'Look, Mala *Boudi*, they're well known to us. They are filthy; they are low born; they do not have choices; they can do anything' – Shefali states these words in a single breath.

'Stop Shefali. Do you want to say that they can only do, because they belong to lower-caste?'

'That is correct, *Boudi*. Will you bring up that low-caste daughter?' – Shefali asks after a little pause. 'I recommend that you take the baby to the police station.'

'No one's caste is written on their skin. Nobody is born into a low-caste family. Besides, we should be unconcerned about whether she was born into a low or high caste. She has now become our daughter. I'm not going to talk to you any longer; you should leave now.'

Ratna has remained silent so far. She was simply paying attention to what they were saying. She's now exploding.

'Mala *Boudi*, law does not allow you to call her your daughter.'

'I'm aware of that, Ratna. I also have idea how it happens. Therefore, you shouldn't worry about it. Allow us to concentrate on our own business.'

Shefali and Ratna are a little depressed as they leave Mala's house.

'Have you noticed Mala *Boudi's* behaviour, Shefali? She is so arrogant that she will not step foot on the ground.'

'You're absolutely correct, Ratna. Had she not been a barren herself?'

Mukulesh is lying on the bed after lunch, and Mala is stroking the baby in her lap.

Mala is completely unaware that Babli has arrived and taken a position behind her. Returning her gaze, Mala spots Babli and inquires, 'Thakurji, when have you arrived?'

'I've been here for a while. You were so preoccupied with the infant that you were completely unaware of my presence.'

'No, that is not the case,' Mala states emphatically.

'Shefali rang me up in the morning. She said that you've brought a baby home.'

Mukulesh says, 'Yes, I wanted to let you know but I couldn't get around to it.'

'It's pointless to talk about it. Tell me – where have you found the baby?'

'You should talk to each other and I am going to get some tea and snacks for Thakurji.' Laying the baby in the lap on the bed, Mala makes her way towards the kitchen. As Mukulesh watches Mala leave the room, he adds, 'Make a wonderful cup of tea and bring it for me, but......' Mukulesh then remarks, throwing his gaze on Babli…'I got the baby in front of Tumpa's house.'

'Don't you think that they had thrown the baby over there?'

'It may or may not be.'

'Dada, what you say! It seems to me that it is their activity. According to what I've heard, Tumpa leaves his house every day and comes back the following day.'

'Yes, she works in a nursing home as a nursemaid.'

'It's just an excuse to go to a nursing home. This is her baby.'

Mala enters with *Luchis* and sweets.

'*Boudi*, you have cooked so much!' Babli takes a sip of tea and says, 'I will not have all these items.'

The high-ups of the society are present. Tumpa and Tumpa's mother are seated behind everyone, ill at ease since everyone is looking at them with suspicion. Who knows what fate has in store for them? As a result, they have fear written all over their faces. Tumpa's eyes are dripping with tears. Their appearances are emblazoned with curiosity. Someone in the crowd gets up and says – 'Do you all know why you have come?'

'Yes, everyone says together.'

Then he casts a slanted glance towards Mukulesh *Babu*. Mukulesh *Babu* has a calm demeanour. Thereby, he maintains a steady gaze while sitting with a firm heart.

'Mukulesh Babu, I have heard you had the baby in the neighbourhood where Tumpa's house is located.' Amrendra *Babu's* voice seems to be laden with irony.

'Yes, you have heard that right.'

'So, I'm guessing it's their activity?'

'No, no, no.' Tumpa screams, 'It's a lie, and all of this is a fabrication!'

'These are not lies,' Amlesh *Babu* retorts with a scowl on his face. 'Do you believe we're all clueless of what's going on?' he inquires. 'You go out every afternoon and come back the next day. What are your plans, dear?'

'As a nursemaid, I work in a nursing home. I work entire night.'

'Are we supposed to believe everything you say?' For well-bred, ethical ladies, such behaviour is unthinkable.'

Tumpa sobs hysterically as she breaks down. Her mother pulls her close to her. 'You guys have brought us to justice in an erroneous manner,' she asserts firmly, standing up. 'We haven't made any mistakes.'

'It's only natural that as the girl's mother, you would try your hardest to conceal your daughter's failings. But you wouldn't be able to stay here any longer. You would lose contact with everyone in the village if you stayed here. It's now up to you whether you want to stay here or go somewhere else.'

'We are getting along, but we would not stand such false allegations,' Tumpa's mother says, taking her daughter's hand in hers. 'The genuine perpetrator will be exposed one day. Let's go, Tumpa. Let's go somewhere else for the time being.' While getting ready, they overhear someone saying something.

'The family subsists on the girl's ill-gotten money; she's talking big here.'

'What exactly is death?' Another makes a caustic remark.

Amrendra *Babu*, happy at their exit, asks – 'What have you decided, Mukulesh *Babu*? What do you have in mind for the baby? Take her to the nearest police station.'

'No way, we're going to raise her.' She is my child.' In a stern tone, Mala says.

'Exactly what are you saying? Do you know what caste the infant belongs to? If she is Tumpa's daughter, she is the daughter of a fisherwoman. That is not appropriate, Mukulesh *Babu*. The Brahmins have taken in a fisherman's daughter! No, it isn't correct. Religion is very important in society. As a result of your conduct, you will lose respect and value.'

'Let me think about that, Bhattacharya sir. I don't give a damn if she's from the lower or upper castes. We'll pay for her education and adopt her after she finishes school. 'Don't get fired up over it.'

– It's midnight on the eve of New Year's Eve. The sky is overcast. There is nothing but darkness as far as the eye can see. With the baby, they sleep beside the window. Mukulesh is startled awake. At the window, a slight shadow appears.

'Can you tell me who's there?'

'Could you just tell me what happened?' When Mala wakes up and sits up in bed, she is startled.

'There was someone standing by the window, Mala.'

'How do you respond? If there was someone there, where has he gone? I'm not sure what you observed while sleeping. Splash some water on your face with a glass.'

Mukulesh rises from his bed and walks over to the sink, where he wets his face.

Mala, on the other hand, makes an effort to disregard the impending incident, but a nagging uncertainty remains in her mind. Mukulesh's mind is racing with questions: whom has he seen? Who could have shown up here? There's a new visitor on the way. She hasn't settled into a good sleep routine in general. Mala notices something outside the window and stares at it for a long time. Then she spots a bogie draped in a cloth approaching the window.

The bogie begins to back away as soon as Mala sits up. Mala softly pokes Mukulesh and says, 'Listen! Wake up, wake up!'

'What has happened?'

'I have seen him.'

'Whom?' Mukulesh sits up on the bed, stumbling.

'I've seen the same person you saw that day.'

'Mala, what's the matter? Who comes to this place on a regular basis? And what brings him here?'

'Surely, he has a motive.'

'I think so.'

'We must keep track of who comes here on a daily basis. We won't be able to sleep today. Turn off the lights and retire to your bed. I'll return to the rear door and remain there. If you detect anything strange, please let me know.'

The evening is drawing to a close. After a long wait, Mukulesh is standing near the door. Today, no one is visible.

'Mala, I believe, that no one will show up today.'

'Shush, shush! Take a look at that.........'

The bogey gradually approaches the window's side. The whole body of the bogey is encased in burqa. Opening the door Mukulesh creeps towards the bogey and asks in a hushed tone – 'who are you?'

The bogey shudders a little bit. It does not utter a single word.

'Say something. Otherwise, I'll summon everyone to a meeting.'

Mala lit up the light of the room by the time. The newcomer takes off his face cloth.

'Shashoti, are you here? Why are you here?'

Shashoti did not go to college that day. Sitting in the resting room, she was watching TV. Shashoti comes out of the room at the sound of the calling bell.

'Is sir present there in the house?' – A 23-24 years old young man stands at the gate and enquires.

'No, dad is not home. But you can sit; dad will come back in a moment.' Siraj pauses for a few moments before entering the room behind Shashoti.

'Please take a seat.'

While sitting on the sofa, Siraj says – 'I am Siraj and what's about you?'

'I am Shashoti.'

That day, he was getting ready to go to college. The sound of the doorbell prompts her to open it. Siraj is waiting in front of the door, holding Shashoti's father's freshly published book *The Same Heart*.

'Are you here?'

'Yes, I've wandered in. Sir's book has a lot of appeal for me.'

'Yes, my father's novel has received a lot of positive feedback from readers. Many letters have also come from Bangladesh. Dad has been rewarded as well.'

'In fact, I would not have known much about Sir if I hadn't been able to read this book. Sir is also a decent human being. My admiration for Sir has grown as a result of reading this novel.'

'I too have appreciated this book. I've got to know my father all over again. I've discovered a lot about my father.'

Since then, Siraj has paid numerous visits to Shashoti's home. He develops a friendship with Shashoti's parents. When he bit by bit took a place in Shashoti's mind, she was unaware of it.

'Siraj, will your parents accept me?'

'My mother knows nothing but me. My happiness, she says, is her happiness. She claims that whoever I marry will be everything to her.'

'Does your father hold the same opinion?'

'Perhaps he does not share my viewpoint. He will not, however, turn his back on my mother.'

'I am not sure about my mother. But I have no problem with my father. As far as my father is concerned, I do not need to take tension.'

'Then why are you making late?' Siraj tells with a laugh.

'Will I not complete my studies? You must have a job. Everything will run smoothly after that.'

'Isn't it true, Shashoti, that if I don't obtain a job, everything will be proven wrong?'

'Why it is so? We are in love with each other.'

Bijoy *Babu* has returned home a little early today. Bijoy *Babu* asks Devika Devi, 'Where is Shashoti, Devika?' as soon as she enters the house with the tray of tea in her hand. Devika says as she places the cup of tea on the table, 'She has gone out for a little while.'

'Where?'

'Siraj visited our house and she has gone out with him. Why has she gone with Siraj?' Her friendship with Siraj is growing stronger. Devika Devi has been contemplating this for some time. She, on the other hand, remains silent and continues to pour tea into the cup.

'Why aren't you speaking up?'

'How should I respond?'

'Are you oblivious to anything? You're a mother, after all. Listen, I don't like their hanging out so frequently.'

Bijoy *Babu* and Devika Devi have both gone out for a short while. Shashoti is alone at home. She has returned home from college a while ago. Half-lying on the sofa, Shashoti is having a quick skim through a magazine.

The ringing of the beckoning bell irritates her. He opens the door, a little irritated.

'Oh you?' Shashoti's face lights up with a smile.

'I've arrived,' Siraj replies, a smile on his face.

'You have done well.'

'Let's go on an outing.'

'No, no, my parents are not home. We should exchange pleasantries at home today.'

It is eleven o'clock at night but her parents have not returned home yet. Shashoti is lying face down on the pillow. Siraj has gone away quite a while ago. What happened to Shashoti today?

'Siraj..........'

'Tell me.......'

'You know Siraj, every human being dreams; human being loves to dream; I also love to dream. Do you not love to dream, Siraj?'

'Who says that I don't like to dream? Isn't it true that everyone loves to dream?'

'Yes. This is something that every human being does. Does everyone's dream come true, Siraj?'

'I don't know. Their dreams may or may not come true.'

'Dreams are dreams, Shashoti. Dreams have no resemblance to reality. That's why it is referred to as a dream.'

'Yet why do people dream?'

'They dream because it is something they enjoy doing.'

'Shit! Electricity has gone off? You should remain in your current position. I am going to light the candle.'

'Hey Shashoti. Have you managed to locate the candle?'

'Yeah, I have got it. But I have not found the matches.'

'I have a lighter. You come forward with the candle.'

The room is bathed in a lovely mellow light. Siraj casts a glance at Shashoti. She appears to be a magician in the light of a candle.

The candle is still in the hand of Shashoti. Siraj approaches her slowly, his hand on his chin. She shudders softly. She forgets to put the candle in the candlestick. Siraj says softly – 'will you keep holding the candle in your hand?' After being embarrassed, she put the candle in the candlestick. They sit side by side on the sofa; then no one knows when they took off the boundation and everything got turned upside down; an intense feeling gradually germinates all over their bodies and they get lost in another world. They appear to be carried away to a dreamland by the rough sea waves. The calling bell rings. Exhausted, she walks towards the door and opens it.

'Shashoti, did you fall asleep? I've been ringing the bell for quite some time.'

'No – I simply dozed off.'

'Are you feeling weak? Do you have fever?'

Devika Devi gets busy and walks towards Shashoti, trying to measure the temperature of her with her hands on her body.

'No, mom, I am doing well.'

'But your face looks very dry.'

'That's not the case; mom, change the cloths. By then, I'll have the dinner ready.'

Noon ends and afternoon begins then afternoon ends and evening begins. Shashoti is lying on the bed. She is exhausted today.

'Shashoti..... Shashoti...... are you still sleeping? It is now evening time, so get up.'

'Mom......' Shashoti calls.

'What has happened Shashoti?' Bijaya Devi shudders at the voice of Shashoti. She goes to her daughter.

'Mom, mom....' Shashoti hugs her mother and cries.

'Why are you crying? Tell me what has happened.'

'Mom, I've made an awful mistake.'

'What kind of blunder have you made?' Mother's throat trembles with a panic she doesn't understand.

'I'm going to have a child.'

'Can you tell me what you've said? She is stunned and glued to the spot.

'Siraj came here...... He wants to marry me.'

'How do you think that's possible? How have you made this blunder? They belong to Muslim community; if we accept him our society will never accept him. Besides, your father will never agree to this marriage.'

'No mom. You inform and persuade him.'

Devika is unable to sleep while lying in bed. Bijoy *Babu* is in fast asleep. Devika Devi climbs out of bed. She takes the glass of water from the table in her hand, drinks it all in one swallow, and then sets the glass down. Bijoy *Babu* is awakened by the dim bulb's soothing light.

'What's happened? Why are you there?'

'I am not feeling sleepy.'

'Give a little splash of water in your eyes and you will feel drowsy.'

She lies down on the bed, her head resting on the pillow. 'I am not feeling sleepy.'

'Are you paying attention to what I'm saying?'

'What's happened?'

'I want to say something?'

'What do you want to say? Is there any problem if you say it tomorrow?'

'Our Shashoti...'

'What Shashoti?' She remains silent.

'Why are you silent?'

'You will get angry. That's why I am afraid to say.'

'What are you talking about? Please hurry up and say whatever it is you want to say.'

'Our Shashoti is going to be a mother.'

He sat up in bed pondering internally 'Who is that guy who has dared to harm to such an extent?'

'Siraj wants to marry her.'

'What? That coward one? How dare he do such a thing?'

'Right away, I......'

'So late at night?'

'Yes. At this hour of the night........ Shashoti, Shashoti?' Devika pursues him.

The train is available early in the morning. He gives stern instructions that Devika Devi and Shashoti should stay there for a few months. That is the house in a village. Sometimes they should come here on a summer vacation. Pachu stays here with his family since a long time. A house with a tin canopy and brick walls has been built for him. Shashoti's body has grown in size. She stands in front of the mirror and examines herself in great detail. Her body and mind get filled with an unidentified happiness. She recalls his father's dreadful expression, a face she had never seen before in her life. 'Siraj is a Muslim; your marriage with him will never be possible. Be prepared to atone for the mistakes you have made.'

She cannot match this father with the father she had known for so long. She recalls the events of that day. There was a huge public gathering. Shashoti's father was adorned with garlands on the stage. He is Bijoy Sanal, an author from our village, for whose greeting this event has been planned. He has added a new dimension to literature. Who can show an example of such a liberal mentality of secularism? In his novel, Bijoy *Babu* has set a great example by bringing Hindu and Muslim into the bond of marriage. We are happy to reward him. Amrendra *Babu*, a well-known social worker, is enthralled. The meeting room reverberates with huge applause. Devika Devi and Shashoti have come back home in the morning today. Shashoti is now feeling lighter. But she is yet to see the person who has been keeping her burdened.

Mala now stands in front of Shashoti with the baby. She pushes the child towards him and says, 'hold.' Shashoti stretches her hands out to catch her baby but draws back.

With lightning speed, she takes a three-foot step back. She inquires, 'Have you seen Siraj? Siraj......' Where has he vanished to? Then she begins to walk backwards, as if she were a wanderer.

****

8

Realisation

Tarik Anowar

Manisha hasn't seen a field in a long time. She has never seen the pond's black water. Animesh has built a house in Madhyamgram. In his backyard, there is a large area of empty land. There are various flowering plants which Manisha has planted there, including Chinarose, Gandharaj, Tuberose, Rose, Jasmine, Jasminum Sambac, and a variety of trees. In the garden, Chrysanthemum and Dahlia are still blooming on the edge of winter. Manisha pulls up a chair and sits among the trees. The spring south wind catches her in the face, nose, and possibly the core of her heart. She doesn't seem to be afflicted by the passage of time. She seems to have the same green heart that she did as a child. A human heart, in most cases, does not desire to age. Manisha does not want to die; hence she does not want to get old. Manisha wishes to experience the glitz and glam of this world in fresh ways. Manisha would swim in the lake's murky water, frequently astonishing everyone with her dive-swimming. She would suddenly hold up her head as she dived into the water. She would lift her head from the water and smile distantly when everyone was thinking about her.

'Hey, you've been sitting in water for so long; now it's time for you to go to school.' Manisha is unconcerned by her mother's advice. She swims in her own unique style. She emerges from the water and hurries as her mother's reprimand grows louder.

'What's the matter, and why are you in such a hurry?'

'As you can see, Dad, Mom forbids me from swimming.'

Now, the spoiled daughter of the father begins to make excuses. 'So much swimming will make you sick,' Nirmalendu *Babu* tells his daughter, disregarding his wife's warning.

Manisha had already gone to the bathroom to change her clothes. Nirmalendu *Babu* is a high school assistant headmaster in a village outside of Kolkata. He is well-known for his work as a mathematics instructor. Teachers are given special consideration because this is a local school. Nirmalendu *Babu* is an immigrant from East Bengal. After two or three years of the partition of the country in 1947, he came to India. After the partition, there were riots between the Hindus and the Muslims. Many houses were burnt, many lives were lost prematurely.

'Didn't you hear about the Muslim riot? So, Nirmalendu *Babu*, you won't get it. I abandoned my homeland because of Muslims. Is it a little annoying distraction? I had to leave East Bengal behind for them.'

'Well, Pandit Ji, tell me that only Muslims are to blame for the rioting. Hadn't the Hindus taken part in it as well?'

'Talking to you is meaningless. You don't see anything wrong with Muslims.'

'Why do you become angry? Listen, they are not as much to blame for the riot as politicians, particularly British politicians. They are the ones who started the riot between Hindus and Muslims and then fled. They've divided the golden Bengal into two halves. We're wandering like nomads these days.'

'We are indeed roaming.' You have made an excellent point. However, Hindu-Muslim riots have been going on for a long time. Muslims, on the other hand, are unable to tolerate Hinduism.'

'Pandit Ji, the reverse is also true. Some politicians have created religions for their own gain throughout history. Pandit Ji, in modern times, when science has enabled men to go to the Moon and Mars, yet religious dogmas of the same faith continue to pervade the minds of these modern people. That should not have happened this way, but that is the truth. We still, to some extent, blindly follow ancient customs without questioning them. Due to certain religious dogma, we are repeatedly losing our way. We're losing our hands and legs, and we're becoming paralysed. Do you know what's causing it? 'There is a lack of consciousness and knowledge.'

'People are no longer as illiterate as they once were. They basically learn to gain knowledge.' 'Yes, they do. Traditional education, however, while it literally educates individuals, it does not necessarily build consciousness in them. Consciousness and knowledge acquisition is not the same thing. Acquiring knowledge entails learning about something, whereas consciousness entails fully comprehending the essence of something. There is a significant difference between the two. Furthermore, the majority of students do not adhere to basic educational principles. Most of the time, they study in order to find work.'

'You're entirely correct. Studying does not always imply getting a decent career.'

'Not only that. It's to expand the range of our thoughts and awareness. This inconsistency will stay with them until they can find the source of genuine knowledge. This heinous riot will most likely continue until then.'

'Will there be a riot?'

'Yes, it will'.

'Sir Ji, why?'

'Because one clan will definitely try to sway the other. Different religious organisations will be enticed to gain political benefit for their vested interests in this way. Do you not see the many political parties, such as the Congress and the C.P.M.? They, too, are distinct religions.

They, too, have political goals in mind. In the not-too-distant future, they may be called religions.'

'Gentlemen, you are destroying religion and political parties. It's pointless to speak with you.' Pandit Ji was enraged and sweating profusely, so he pulled off his shirt and held it in his hand before putting it on his soldier. He finally made his way back to his house.

Manisha has been stirred up by her father's superstition-free heart since she was a toddler. She misses her father a lot at times.

'Manisha…'

'Yes, Papa.'

'Today there is Saraswati puja at school, Manisha. You will go there, isn't it?'

'Yes, I will, father. But…'

'But what?'

'Father, the clay idol appears to me to be nothing more than clays. It doesn't make sense to me.'

'You are correct, Manisha. These aren't even close to being useful. Your strength comes from your capacity to remain stable.

Your focus and concentration will help you achieve your goal. Isn't the story *Mantrashakti* on your syllabus?'

'Yes, father. I've read it.'

'*Mantras* and incantations don't exist,' says the author. When a professional fighter takes up a stick in his hand, he gets dedicated to it. As a result, no one can overpower him. Mother, you should realise that fear is at the base of everything. Man cannot accept his imminent death in any form. That terror is the source of the prayers. So people pray because they are afraid of dying; for example, fear of snakes has given rise to *Mansha puja*, and fear of spring has given rise to *Sheetala puja*, and so on.'

Like her father, Manisha can't think of clay idols as something extraordinary. It seems to her only clay statue. But all her friends are different. They would get up early in the morning after having a bath and head to school. They'd be holding a flower-tray with a variety of colourful flowers on it. They'd fast for the entire day. They would next make flower and bael leaf offerings in front of the idol. Manisha felt compelled to make an offering with her friends all of the time. When the flower and bael leaves had fallen from her grasp, she couldn't understand why. And she had the impression that this clay statue had no force. Furthermore, she questioned why they were had to chant the *mantras* in Sanskrit. Are their priests unable to communicate in Bengali? Her beliefs and ideas did not match those of her friends. Gradually, the gap between her and her friends widens. And she was a little hurt because of that. She was gnawed by a terrible loneliness. Manisha had the impression that her pals were much happier if they could delegate all of their obligations to their fictional idol. They didn't have to deal with the harsh reality.

'I am very fond of your prayers, Manisha.'

'See, Lutfa, I told you before and I'll tell you again: I don't have any prayers.'

'Why not? You're a Hindu, right? Hindus have a lot of prayers, don't they?'

'Could it be?'

'Then?'

'Then what?'

'Why don't you have?'

'As we are not Hindus?'

'Then what?'

'Human being.'

'We all are human beings. Still ……'

"Listen, Lutfa, I'm not a believer in any religion, not Muslim, Hindu, Christian, or anything else. I am only a human being, Lutfa. And a human being has no religion.'

Manisha is in tenth grade. In her mind, religious intricacies gradually take root. No one is immune to religious rigidity, whether they be Muslims, Hindus, or Christians. Lutfa was unable to participate in any of the prayers that day. She was not permitted to participate, despite her strong desire to do so. They, too, have several theological justifications and orthodox views. For the Eid festival, people fast for a month without drinking even water throughout the day, severely punishing their bodies. Manisha believes that there should be no religion everywhere on the planet, and that a human being should be recognised solely as a human being. Manisha's heart is sometimes heavily burdened. Manisha's heart was broken that day by Lutfa's actions. The Eid festival was lavishly celebrated in Lutfas' home on that day. There was a halo of light all around us. However, she did not have the luck of sharing the supper with her companion. She had to sit somewhere else.

'Lutfa, why did you give me a banana leaf to eat my dinner on?'

'You are not to eat from our plate.'

'Why?'

'We are Muslims,' she says. 'It will be our sin if we give you our dish to eat from.'

'Will it be sin? Why?'

'I'm not sure. That's what my mum says.'

'Fie, Lutfa! Such words are not appropriate for your mouth. You're not like everyone else. You're concentrating on your studies. Human beings are made of similar flesh and blood, as you are well aware.'

'As you can see, Manisha. I'm not sure how much I comprehend. Mother said, Give, and I did.' "You're not supposed to do whatever your mother says. Will you not make an effort to understand anything? I'm going to eat off your plate. Let's see how much you lose.'

Manisha takes a bite out of Lutfa's plate.

'Manisha, you shouldn't have done it.'

A *Kali* idol was discovered at the point of the shovel while digging the ground for a pond at Lutfas' residence. They were Hindus, low-caste Hindus; it is said, two or three generations ago. Due to the oppression of upper-caste Hindus, they embraced Islam in groups. Most Muslims in East and West Bengal were low-caste Hindus before becoming Muslims. Their low-caste identity does not go away, whether they are Muslims, Hindus, Buddhists, Christians, or anyone else. This is how the majority of low-caste Hindus has converted. However, their marginalisation still continues in all religions. Religious dogma has drained Manisha's heart. She believes that everyone on the earth should be recognised as one and the same. In the same sense, they might have had a fraternal bond. Manisha despises all religions. A human being, she believes, is just that: a human being. The theological war is a fight between factions. The more civilised a man becomes; the larger his group's peripheral becomes. Miracles and blind faiths are still deeply embedded in our hearts today. Manisha is well aware that many people are enamoured with saints and monks, and that they are often fleeced as a result of their naive faith in superstition.

'I'm going to school drenched in rain today.'

'I will show you a ghost.'

'Are you willing to display a ghost?' Madhuchhanda and Madhumita asked in unison.

'Yes, it's an alive ghost.' To avoid getting wet in the rain, roll the books snugly in plastic and place them in the bag. 'Now is the time to fold your umbrella.'

'What makes you think I'm going to fold the umbrella?' 'I'm going to be drenched.'

'Because we're going to get wet, I told you to wrap the books in plastic.' Manisha pulls her hand back and adds, 'This is where the pistol is.'

Classes were currently in progress. They proceeded towards the class on foot. The names were being called out by the teacher at the time. With his large eyes, he glanced at them.

'You are fully soaked. You are not obliged to attend class today. You will inform the matron and go back home once the rain has stopped.'

Manisha gives a small chuckle. The rain stops after a while, and Manisha says, 'Let's go now.'

'Where?'

'To keep an eye on a ghost.'

'Can you tell me where it is?'

'At Guruma's residence,'

'What?'

'You will see once you go.'

The rain seemed to pick up speed once more. The sky was filled with dark clouds, rumbling of thunder and flashes of lighting creating an eerie atmosphere all around. Manisha had a good time. The road got waterlogged. Dipping her feet in water was very enjoyable for her. To get to Guruma's residence, they must cross a canal. Madhumita takes a step forward towards the wooden bridge. Manisha takes her hand in hers. They're staring at the bamboo bridge. They will go through it.

'We will have much fun, won't we?'

'Why, the wooden bridge is better, let's go through it.'

'It's not easy to walk with you, Madhuchhanda. Now I see I have to walk alone. However, Subhra is brave. Who is aware of her absence from school today? Manisha moves in the direction of the bamboo bridge. Being compelled, they follow her.

Manisha had been intrigued by Guruma's dreadlocks for a few days. In addition, there is a sizable audience, a queue of cars, and their mound of fruits. Manisha observes how the weak and handicapped are assisted in exiting the vehicle and transported to Guruma's home. Why do they travel? Manisha had heard that Guruma can cure someone's illness by reciting water and oil. Is Guruma really able to heal them? Why do they go if not? How do individuals come to believe in the treatment she recites? So, these are of a higher level than medical treatment. Manisha believes that Guruma takes advantage of the weak and vulnerable. Actually, these patients' illnesses are beyond the scope of medicine. People with weak hearts will readily cling to a miracle in the hopes of curing their loved ones. Opportunity seekers like Guruma mercilessly deceive them every day by seizing on their vulnerabilities.

'Hey listen, move cautiously. Everyone is sleeping soundly. If you make any noise, they will awaken.'

'Manisha, where is ghost?'

'Hush, gently. Why do you get so busy? Hold on, you'll see it. In order to show you, I haven't been able to see it yet. Come into the veranda with me.'

'Look, the ghost is there!' Manisha abruptly said.

'Where?'

'There…'

That is, in fact, dreadlock.

'Guruma's head is tied with that. I concurred. That is a false set of dreadlocks. Guruma actually sports the artificial dreadlocks.'

It does, yes. If not, how does Guruma get this treatment?

'So, Manisha, is it your fault?' said Madhumita.

'Hush, hush, slowly.' Manisha said, picking up her dreadlocks with both hands, 'Now I shall go to school once.'

Everyone was shocked to see Burima's dreadlocks that day. Before wind, the news had reached every corner. Guruma's impact subsequently diminished.

Manisha didn't attend college today. She is curled up in bed. The history book is held in front of her eyes.

'Manisha, I want you to major in science.'

'No, dad. I'll research the past.' He was a little disappointed, but he didn't stop her.

'Your mother wants you to become a doctor when you grow up, you know, daughter.'

'And yours...' Manisha said lightheartedly.

Nirmalendu *Babu* doesn't say anything at all.

Manisha gives her dad a hug.

Manisha's train of thinking is interrupted by the calling bell. She puts the book down and peers through the door to find Lutfa.

'What's wrong, Lutfa? You seem quite pleased today.'

'It's my wedding,' she said.

'What does your marriage signify? Is an exam coming up?' Without letting her finish the word Lutfa said – 'Hmm, it has been fixed. Besides, Sahajada is going to Bangladesh.'

'Sahajada is your maternal cousin?'

'Yes, so he wants to complete the marriage before going.'

'Is it also your brother's wedding? Are you and your brother getting married on the same day?'

'I'm getting married to Sahajada. You must arrive.' Quickly, Lutfa says it. Manisha did not attend the wedding reception. She was unable to accept the union of a brother and a sister. Don't they realise that marriages between close relatives carry the risk of deformed and disabled births? It is axiomatic as long as the religion permits it. Still, Sahajada? He is a doctor and a science student. How he comes to make this error. No solution pops into Manisha's head. The practise of marrying an uncle to a niece is common in Andhra Pradesh as well. Manisha believes that religion plunges a person into a lifeless, airless, and gloomy cave. When the religious goal is achieved, the cave's entrance will be sealed. What a terrifyingly dark cave it is. Manisha trembles from an unidentified terror. She gets the impression that people are tearing and devouring their own flesh in that cave. Despite countless attempts, they are unable to locate the exit.

When Manisha was a B.A. student, she started dating Animesh. One day, Animesh unexpectedly visits Manisha at her home in Goria. Manisha responds to the knocking and opens the door.

'Is it Nirmalendu *Babu's* residence?'

'Yes. I don't precisely recognise you.' Manisha's eyes are full of exclamation.

'I'm Animesh. Animesh smiles sweetly while blushing.

'Are you Animesh *Da*? Is Ganesh uncle your.......'

'Yes, he is my dad.'

'I couldn't recognise you at all.' Manisha is embarrassed a little.

'I also failed to recognise you. Manisha, are you that restless girl? You now appear to be a lady.' 'A lady indeed, as I study in college. Leaving your half pant, you have taken full pant actually. Now you too seem to be a matured man.'

'Exactly.' The two laugh out loudly.

That night Manisha's mother didn't leave Animesh to go without feeding him rice. Animesh's father Ganesh *Babu* and Manisha's father Nirmalendu *Babu* both served as teachers at the same school in the same village for some days. After serving for a couple of years as teachers, Nirmalendu *Babu* picked up a good job and went to

Kolkata. Then Ganesh *Babu* also came to Jadavpur. He got a job of professor at Jadavpur University. After that, Animesh used to come to Manishas' house now and then. Animesh was then a medical student. And Manisha was a college student. Now and then they would bunk college and visit Gorer Math, Victoria Lake, cinema hall and many more places. Probably every human being becomes a mere child at a particular time. An incident of that day makes Manisha laugh.

'Oho, the slipper has been torn.'

'It has torn to go to your hand from your leg, Manisha?'

'I'm in trouble and you make fun of me?'

'No more words. Now take the slipper in your hand and let's go.'Animesh says while buying fried nuts.

'What? Is it possible to walk barefoot?'

'Walk few steps and let us see if it can be mended anywhere.' Even after ransacking, he could not find a cobbler. What a miserable condition Manisha faced! Being compelled, she had to buy a pair of Hawaii slippers and throw the torn one. Even now Animesh sometimes tells Manisha about that incident.

Manisha was sitting on an easy chair in garden. The heat of the sunrays is well there.

'What are you doing in this dark garden during this cold? You will catch cold easily', said Animesh

Truly she could not understand when it has become evening. Being busy, Manisha left the chair and walked towards the house.

'Get ready quickly, Manisha', says Animesh.

'Why?'

'You forgot in the meantime? Didn't Jotirmay come and invite yesterday?'

'O yes, I forgot it totally. Their registry has been done already, hasn't it?'

'Yes, now they will give a party in their house. You've seen the girl, haven't you Manisha?'

'Yes, I've seen. She came with Jotirmay one day, I presume.'

'O yes, that is true?'

'What's her name?'

'Rabeya Khatun.'

'Rabeya too is a doctor, isn't she?'

'Yes. They will go to America after their marriage. They have got their passports.'

'Has their marriage been accepted by their families?'

'Why won't they accept?'

'For the difference between the lower caste and the upper caste raises storm in our society. Besides, their religions are different too?'

'Jotirmay's father Pradip *Babu* is a man of high quality. I respect him. He says that there can't be any rule or obstacle that may derogate the respect of human beings. He says the humanity of a man is his religion. He wholeheartedly hates the orthodoxies of the Hindu religion.'

'That day, he told Animesh that they have become civilised as human being. You know what is the truth? Even now the human being lives in the primitive age. The only difference is that they have learnt to prepare a mask and wear it.'

'I think, uncle, this religious fight is the primitive instinct. We have not been able to control this instinct even a little bit. Perhaps we have not tried. But where is the way of release from this instinct, uncle?'

Pradip *Babu* seems to be serious a little bit. 'Listen, Animesh, man's conscience is the only way of release from this mentality. One needs proper education for this. Most of the students follow rote learning to pass the examination. They don't even know the genuine meaning of education.

Whoever loves the living being?

Is serving God in the real sense.

Forgetting the meaning of these words, they assemble in temple, mosque and church. They drink dirty water called *charanamrita*. After that, even if they die, they take it as the blessing of God. Got it, Animesh? Perhaps mankind wouldn't be able to escape this darkness of ignorance.'

'No, uncle. Science is making a progress rapidly. You'll see one day that all darkness will be eliminated and the human society will be enlightened.'

Rabeya has worn a red sari. She has a smile of happiness on her face. Rabeya moves forward to see Manisha who comes near her. Then Rabeya holds one of Manisha's hands and says, 'you have come too late actually.' Manisha smiles and stretches a bouquet of flowers. Rabeya too smiles. Sparkle of happiness reflects all over her face. No one except Rabeya's brother has accepted this marriage. Jotirmay's relatives except his parents also boycotted this marriage. But some people have come to this marriage ceremony to please their happiness.

'Jotirmay will surely make a rare incident, won't he, Animesh?'

'Yes, Manisha, now it seems to me that the world not only yields to the ignorant but also gives due honour to the wise. That day I had a conversation with Rabeya's brother. His manner of conversation is very well. At least he has some progressive thinking.' Suddenly Animesh becomes a little oblivious. He remembers the incident of that day.

'Sir, it is not right not to observe puja. It is mingled in our blood. *Durga, Kali, and Shib* – these are important for our spiritual life. They talk to many devotees.' Durjay is saying these words very excitedly.

'They talk? Who told you this impossible word?'

'Yes, sir. I have known it from reading the scriptures.'

'Listen, Durjay, clay statue can never talk. Actualy the one who believes that they speak, it is actually the disease of his mind. He thinks so much over it that he loses his balance of thinking power. Normally his nerves become useless. As a result, these awkward incidents occur. And ordinary people take this disease as something miraculous as we know of many devotees, sick with this disease have talked with the statue and that statue, being alive, has also talked with them.'

'That does happen, sir. *Kali* Thakur has talked to Ramkrishna.' Animesh doesn't feel like talking anymore. This boy comes to Animesh to study Physics for two days. Animesh can't understand why he studies Physics? What is he getting out of it? 'Listen, Durjay, he who doesn't understand the reality cannot actually seek knowledge. I don't expect miraculous ideas from you.'

An indescribable pain gnaws at him. The difference of upper and lower rank among people is actually created by some powerful persons. Puja and rituals are also their invention. For their own interest, they have instilled these among human beings so much so that it is very difficult to be released from them. Animesh consoles his depressed heart. Perhaps one day, the germ of this cruel disease will be discovered and being recovered, men will certainly go back to a healthy life. Animesh tosses and turns in the bed. He doesn't feel like sleeping under any circumstance. He gets down from the bed and takes the covered glass of water in his hand from the table. Animesh quaffs some water, then lights a cigar and sits on a chair. Manisha is sleeping profoundly. He goes near her and pulls the shawl up to her throat. It is very cold in the night. The winter is yet to end. Manisha awakes as soon as the shawl is pulled.

'Haven't you slept?'

'I don't feel like sleeping.'

'Why, are you feeling unwell?' Manisha puts hand on her forehead.

'No, nothing like that.'

'Wash your hands and face and lie down on the bed closing your eyes. You will fall asleep.' Animesh switched off the light and put his head on the pillow. Closing his eyes in the dark room, he searches for the shadow of darkness.

Today Manisha has received a letter from Lutfa. Lutfa is in Bangladesh now. She has gone to there after her marriage. Communication with her has been disrupted for many days. Manisha opens the letter lying under the pillow and reads.

Manisha,

I could not get your address even after trying my best. But I needed you tremendously. Suddenly I met Joya in Dhaka. And I got your address. Being in big trouble, I am writing to you. Sahajada has divorced me. I have two daughters – Joriya and Papiya. They live with me. I have been serving in a school for some days. I want my two daughters to study in India. I will go to Kolkata with them soon. Arrange a school and a hostel for them.

Yours

Lutfa

Time travels at its own motion. Manisha and Animesh's only son Deepan studies in Jadavpur Engineering College. Manisha is alone at her home all the time. Sometimes, Lutfa with her daughters comes to visit her. A few days ago, Lutfa finished her life in Bangladesh and came to Kolkata. Now they live at Dumdum in a rented flat. That day

Manisha had arranged the hostel. Keeping her daughters there, Lutfa went to Bangladesh. All their responsibilities were on Manisha. She has fulfilled it in the best possible manner. They have grown up now and are admitted in a college. Cold wind entered from the northern window. She got some injury in her hand while closing the window in a hurry. Manisha was not feeling to get up from bed. Nowadays, she is feeling lethargic in all sort of activities. The Babri Mosque has been demolished a few days ago. A storm of communalism has broken out all over the world. Temples and mosques are burnt in the far Britain also. It seems to Manisha that there has been a renaissance of the Hindu religion. The fight and envy in the name of religion seem to be a primitive instinct. We have not been able to control that instinct properly. Probably we haven't tried in this direction. But where is the way of getting release from this instinct? Manisha's heart is filled with a sort of exhaustion. This time she had to leave the bed for the sound of the calling bell. Joriya enters the room with a bouquet of roses in her hand. 'My M.Sc. result has come out, auntie. I have got first class.' Joriya bows down before Manisha. Manisha lightly embraces Joriya.

'Why didn't Lutfa come, Joriya?'

'Sister is not feeling well, auntie,' Joriya said taking the flower vase in her hand and arranging the flowers in it.

'What will you do now?'

'I would like to do a job.'

'Yes Joriya, every person has to be independent whether a male or a female. In our country, women have less tendency to be independent. They only blame the men for not giving freedom. Actually, all human beings come to this earth in a free and independent state but they don't have this feeling. All are independent by birth. And it is also their duty to protect their independence. Women are habituated to take foods collected by others. If you share somebody else's food, he will surely want to dominate. Actually, girls' conscience has not awakened till now, Joriya. Remember marriage is not the last solution of life. You have studied, stand on your own feet.'

'Auntie, nowadays consciousness has awakened among girls. They dream of becoming independent pacing with men in every walk of life.'

'Joriya, do you know why I have told you these words? It is because of you are different from the ordinary. You don't accept the rule of the fundamentalists. You prioritise humanity over religion. You have an unprejudiced heart that I can see. I have been thinking to tell you something for a long time. I want to be stress-free to give Deepan in your hand. Do you agree, Joriya?' Joriya doesn't speak. She slowly lowers her head. With the both of her hands, Manisha pulls Joriya in her bosom.

'Mom, see whom I have brought.' A girl enters the room following Deepan. 'Mom, haven't I told you about Baishakhi? She is that Baishakhi.

'Baishakhi……? O…..Yes, have you said?' Manisha answers unmindfully. She stared at the clumsy girl standing in the corner of the room.

****

9

The Nest of the Crow

Saddam Saikh

Today is a day of sadness for the entire village. The entire community appears to have been smothered by an icy wind. A few hungry people are walking down the street. When the evening has faded and the night has descended, no one has noticed. The village is dark since the lights have not been turned on. The gathered people muttering hither and thither. Amiyo's friends went to the hospital. The post-mortem report is yet to come. As a result, Amiyo's body has not yet arrived. Amiyo's better half, Sapna is routinely being knocked out. One year ago, they got married. The body is still giving off the fragrance of newness. Amiyo's mother, Bijayadevi has returned back from the hospital yesterday. She had a tumour in her stomach. She has become unconscious and has not come around so far. Doctor *Babu* has come to cure Sapna and Bijayadevi. Bajreshwar *Babu*, Amiyo's father retired from his job last year. He is baffled by what has occurred to Amiyo. He has had a brief conversation with Amiyo a little while ago. He's gone out shopping for puja. He has spent the entire day in the Pujo's pandal. There are still a few days left for the Puja to set in. The construction of the pandal is nearly complete. 'Everything is as it was before; then Amiyo, no… no… no… it can never happen.' Bajreshwar cups his head. There are stories floating around about how Amiyo was hit by a train, suffered a head injury, and had blood clot inside it. His untimely demise seems to have shocked the entire community. Bajreshwar *Babu* got his only son Amiyo married at an early age; he did not even wait for two months after Amiyo had a job. Amiyo first met Sapna at a wedding reception. Sapna was enthralled by his song. What a lovely full voice he has! She frowns and says that 'if someone doesn't have a lovely voice, he won't be able to sing Rabindra sangeet with a melody and rhythm. You must not like me if you only like my singing.'

Sapna buries her head in Amiyo's chest, and a thin shaft of moonlight falls on their bed at that very time.

Bajreshwar *Babu* was first dissatisfied with Sapna's marriage to Amiyo. Sapna's skin color is black and he has an allergy to black color. However, Bajreshwar *Babu* has now been able to overcome this misconception. Because of Sapna's gentleness, his misconception regarding her black colour has been removed. If Sapna went to her father's house for a day, he became restless. The house always remains festive in the presence of Sapna. 'Dad, it's your milk.' Sapna enters the room wearing a pink woven sari. Bajreshwar *Babu* has forbidden her wearing white saris. He is no longer able to look up at Sapna because of this. What sorrow he feels for that young child! What is her age? She recently turned twenty-one years old. He is no longer able to think at this moment. As Sapna was going to cover the milk in the glass, Bajreshwar *Babu's* comments caught her attention.

'O… my daughter-in-law, is it possible to get a job in the office of Amiyo?'

'Yes dad, I have got the job. They have asked me to join the day after tomorrow." Oh well!' Bajreshwar *Babu's* chest lets forth a suppressed sigh. 'I have received a letter from State Bank notifying me of an appointment.' Amiyo almost runs into the house. Vijaya Devi comes out of the room in a hurry. She wraps her arms around her son and squeezes him tightly. Her eyes twinkle with joy. This is her account of that day, when her eyes were burning and she was having an excruciating pain in her chest.

'Vijaya, we want a girl, what do you say?'

'No girl, only boy' – Vijay protests vehemently.

'No girl?'

'We only want boy', Vijaya clasps his hands and hits Bajreshwar *Babu* lightly on the back.

Bajreshwar *Babu* joked, 'Vijaya, I want a girl.'

Finally, a boy enters into Vijaya and Bajreshwar *Babu's* lives.

'Dad...Dad... A kite is tied with thread in Amiyo's hands.' Amiyo leads his father out of the house and into the yard by his hand. 'Please, Dad, assist me in flying the kite into the sky. One day, my kite will drift away to the country of the sun. Is the sun too far away, Dad?'

'Yes, a long distance away.'

'Isn't it possible, Dad, for us to go?'

'You can't possibly go to it, baby. The sun is a blazing ball of fire. But man has been to the moon and brought soil from there. Go to the moon, baby, when you grow up. Become a well-known scientist around the world.'

'Yes, I'll go, dad. One day I'll arrive on the moon's surface, floating on the clouds.'

With bored eyes, Bajreshwar *Babu* glances out. In the distance, a crow's nest can be seen in a fir tree. They were able to construct the nest after numerous efforts. They've been working on the nest for a long time. However, they were unable to construct a nest on a tree branch. The rag is continually tumbling down. It is repeatedly hoisted and lowered. Perhaps they became hopeless by the failure and went elsewhere in the end. One crow is currently perched on the nest. Its plumage has gone white. The level of redness on its face has decreased dramatically. The crow appears to be suffering from some sort of illness. In pursuit of food, the other crow is rushing for the rice that has been sprinkled around the people's kitchen. It's possible that the crow is now sitting on the eggs. The egg will hatch one day, and the young crow's eyes will open a few days later. Then it will flap its wings and travel far, in different directions, through other countries one day. Sapna has been in the job for almost two years now. She is stress-free now that she has left the baby with her grandmother. Bunbun has developed a strong bond with her grandmother. Even after returning home from work, the baby does not spend much time with her mother. Sapna rolled around on the bed for a few minutes before going into the bathroom to freshen up. Sapna received the cup of tea from Vijaya Devi. There was a lot of crowd on the train and bus today. She looks after the boy who is seated on her lap.

After his morning walk, Bajreshwar *Babu* has the habit of heading to the market. He has just got back home. There is tea in the flask on the tea table. He poured tea into a cup and began flipping through the newspaper. 'Listen! Nowadays, the daughter-in-law appears to be changing.' Bajreshwar *Babu* is also noticing a slight change in Sapna. The crimson colour on the lips looks to be brighter nowadays. I don't really like it. Yet he says that 'it is your mental error, Vijaya.'

Vijaya Devi did not say anything at once. It is against her nature to talk too much. Bajreshwar *Babu* looks away at the blue sky that has touched the ground. This side of the window is very open. Not so many houses have been built yet. Some vacant ground remains on the other side of the field, far away. As a result, the blue sky is still visible. The main road runs directly in front of the house. New massive flats have been built on both sides of it. They're all standing there with the yearning to soar above the clouds. I don't like the building made of bricks. The eyes seem to come to a halt. That's why Bajreshwar *Babu* exclusively prefers the rear window the most. However, the area won't be deserted for long. It is as if it wants to swallow everything. He keeps his eyes open for quite a while on the open path under the open sky. Two sparrows perch at the window and the sound of their chirping causes the ears to be painful.

'Listen, that time I told that the daughter-in-law does not work. I don't have a good idea about what happens to a girl of this age. Nowadays she gets home very late at night.' Bijayadevi speaks these words in a single breath. 'Look, Vijaya, this is her youth; everything is possible at this age. Is it possible to override the laws of nature? And what harm does it do, Vijaya, if Sapna likes someone? She will be married to him. Widow marriage is quite prevalent at present time. How would you react if she were your own daughter, Vijaya? Consider it.' Vijaya Devi doesn't say anything and starts scratching the hem of the cloth with her fingernails. The body appears heavier when it grows weary and worn out. Bajreshwar *Babu* is trying to fall asleep as he leans on the bed with his head on the pillow. He stays up all night attempting to capture the silence outside. What purpose does life serve? Life's rule is to make new ones. What then is man's significance? He too must follow the same set of rules because time does not wait for anyone. He discovers no distinction between a mosquito and a human being. It is morning. On the winding path of the window, a red pomegranate seed-sized piece of sunshine has dropped on the bed. He didn't go for his morning walk today. He closes his eyes and lies in bed for a while longer. He is unable to get out of bed. He has decided not to go somewhere today. On this day, Amiyo had given up all his attachments and embarked on a journey to a foreign land. He fixes his gaze on the portrait of Amiyo on the table, which is encased in a steel frame. A deep breath from the chest mixes with the air and makes the air heavier. He gets up and sits on the bed.

After ringing the calling bell that day, he answered the door. Sameer and Sapna enter the room. Bajreshwar *Babu* looks at Sapna with wide-eyed wonder. 'Dad, he is my friend, Sameer Sen. We work in the same office.' Sapna says the words a little faster. As Sameer attempted to touch the feet of Bajreshwar *Babu*, he held his hand, 'no..... no... stay over here.' The chest trembles with an unknown fear, yet he adjusts to everything. Sapna became restless on the day she left with Bunbun, her only descendant. Vijaya has left her alone like a selfish person. She is all by herself today. On the balcony, there was an easy chair. He rested his weight on it. The sun is about to set. On the horizon, the dim light of night can still be seen. In the sky, a couple of stars appeared. Gradually, the entire world was enveloped in darkness. Bajreshwar *Babu* finds this rich blue darkness wonderful. When he heard, 'Dad...' he was taken aback and redirected his focus to the open door. Where will the baby come from? He's turned into the sky's blue star. It's as if Bajreshwar *Babu* believes all of the stars in the sky are smiling at him.

'Dad, where are you? I'm here.'

'Baby...' he screamed. Godadhor bolts from the kitchen and rushes over to him. Now, this Godadhor is his constant companion.

'What has happened, *Dadababu*?'

'Will you catch hold of me, Godadhor?'

'Oh my God! Your body is burning and you have a fever.' He was taken into the room and placed on the bed by Godadhor. Bajreshwar *Babu* appears to be drowsy. His lips tremble involuntarily. 'Where have you gone, *Dadababu*?'

'*Dadababu*........'

****

10

Topsy-Turvy

Tarik Anowar

Nakulesh *Babu* is not in a good mood today. He doesn't feel like going for a morning walk so he prefers to lie in bed and close his eyes.

'What's up with you, you're still lying down? Are you not feeling well?' Sraboni puts her hand on her husband's forehead.

'No, nothing happened to me.' Nakulesh *Babu* gets up from the bed.

Sraboni casts a quick glance at her husband. 'Don't be dejected,' she advises, 'put the past behind you. We tried no less. For each subject, he had a teacher assigned to him. However, what can be done if he deceives?'

'But, Sraboni, I wouldn't be able to appear in public! If my co-workers in the office find out, my face would fall in disgrace.'

'What else can be done? You have to tell the truth.'

'I did not imagine that Tanmoy would botch up the final exam.'

'It was beyond me. Nothing is left to let the neighbours see our faces. How will we go out of the house? Last year, after Biplob had passed his final exam with better scores in four subjects, his mother sent a pot of sweets.'

'What about us? We are busy hiding our faces.'

'What to do, it was predetermined by our fate. Get out of bed and get ready for breakfast now; don't stay in bed any longer. The tea has already been made, and it seems that it is already cold.' At the tea table, Nakulesh *Babu* is utterly silent. He is peacefully seated. The newspaper is still open and lying on the table. He didn't even touch it. He takes one sip of the cold tea and then quietly exits the house through the front door while holding the market bag in his hand. He had a big dream about his son. He now stands no chance of being admitted into any college. 'I didn't let him experience any lack of anything.' Six teachers were appointed for him. For him, six teachers were chosen. His mother used to accompany him to such tutorial teachers according to the schedule. Tanmoy, however, has completely tarnished their reputation. He no longer has the honour to face his co-workers in the office. Last year, Romesh *Babu's* son completed the final test with letter grades in two subjects. He celebrated his happiness by distributing sweets to everyone. But Tanmoy, he has completely wrecked his prestige. Nakulesh *Babu's* eyes are filled with tears in sorrow and anger. He wipes his eyes with his handkerchief. He is so absorbed in thought that he is completely oblivious of his movement towards market. The falling tears bring him back to the reality.

Nakulesh *Babu* takes Metro train from Dumdum to Central Station and from there he goes to his office on foot. Today he is not feeling well, so he decides to go to his office by bus. As soon as he left the metro station, he saw a large crowd.

'Hello *Dada*, I am telling you. Don't go this way, better you follow that way.' Someone says it to Nakulesh *Babu*.

'*Dada*, what is happening there?'

'An anti-reservation protest is going on.'

Nakulesh *Babu* advances a short distance before discovering the group of students across the street. All vehicle movement has been stopped. A protest against the reservation policy in medical science has been organised by all of the Medical and Nilratan College students. He is obliged to walk the long way.

'What's wrong? You're late too, Nakulesh *Babu*, like me? He is about to be approached by Anirban *Babu*, who is grinning widely.

'Yes, I was late leaving. I'm not feeling well. I had planned to take the bus to get to the workplace, but all the buses are standing right here.'

'Yes, all doctors are in fact protesting against the reservation scheme. Nakulesh *Babu*, such movement is unquestionably justified.'

'Yes, of course.' Nakulesh *Babu* answers with great interest. 'But the government is in favour of the reservation policy.'

'How important is it? The individuals on the reservation list are all incompetent. If they become doctors through the reservation category, they will murder people splitting their chests instead of operating on their stomachs.'

'Yes Anirban *Babu*, you are right. Scheduled Cates and Scheduled Tribes have been enjoying the benefits of reservation policy for a long time and now the OBCs are also included in that category to enhance their numbers.'

'It is really surprising the way sons of peasantry want to study Medical Science and Engineering in reservation category, instead of doing agricultural activities like sowing paddy and harvesting crops. They want to make a topsy-turvy of the conventional social system that has been existing since long. They want to make this reservation policy long-lasting.'

'However, I heard that Dalit people also marched on the streets in favour of this reservation policy. Almost five or six thousand people joined in that march. There was a musical instrument with them which is called *Danka*. Its tune is not pitiful, but very serious.'

'The slogan of their protest was 'Intelligence is inherent in human being. It is never rooted in man-made caste discrimination."

'I have also heard that they organised a huge procession. However, neither the television nor the newspapers covered it.'

'Why Media will promote them? They don't care them. Even the media is working against policy on reservation.'

'That is the only hope. Otherwise, we won't be treated with respect. Can't you notice how the village's children, who were never taught anything other than agricultural land, nowadays consistently display excellent performance. They can no longer be stopped if they continue to take advantage of the reservation policy.'

'You are correct; awareness-raising efforts are needed to ensure that the reservation system is abolished. Otherwise, lower caste pupils will grab anything that cannot be permitted to go on at all. In addition, a terrible catastrophe will strike in our private lives. Do you realise that the ripe coconuts on the tree are about to turn grey, yet we are unable to locate any men of low caste to chop them down? Earlier low-caste people would roam for cleaning the leaves of coconut trees. However, it is really difficult to find them these days.'

'My wife has also been telling to harvest the coconuts for some days. The season of Puja has almost arrived, but the coconuts are not yet harvested. In fact, they are not visible around. If now this is the situation, then who will harvest our coconuts in case they are enlightened with education? Mangoes, blackberries and all other kinds of fruits are generally being harvested by them.'

'Truly, for all these reasons, we need to cooperate with the protesters against the reservation policy.'

'Yes, obviously.'

The meritorious students will be rewarded today at a club in Mukules *Babu's* locality. The members of that club have planned a cultural event for this particular day. Mukules *Babu* was invited as the club's chief guest two days ago. Someone touches his feet as he approaches the stage. Mukules *Babu* observes him with incredulous eyes.

'I am Palash.'

Palash is the son of Kajol. His mother is working as a maid at Nakulesh *Babu's* house. When Palash was a child, he went to his house holding his mother's hand for many times. Nakulesh *Babu* could not recognise him.

'Who are you?'

'I am Palash. I went to your house with my mother in my childhood.'

'Who is your mother?'

'Kajol, the woman who serves as a maid in your house.'

'Okay!' Nakulesh *Babu* moves towards the stage. The anchor's voice echoes throughout the room as the programme is about to begin.

'We would like to greet our chief guest with a garland at the beginning of our award ceremony programme. Nakulesh Chattopadhyay, our chief guest and the most revered person in our locality, will be greeted by our younger sister Malobika by donning flowers.' The ceremonial premises reverberate with applause.

'Now, it is the time to distribute the prizes. For the first prize, we request Palash Halder to come on the stage. This year Palash has passed the Secondary Examination by securing letter marks in three subjects. Our locality is proud of him.' Nakulesh *Babu* became perplexed in his gaze. What is he looking at! How is it possible to give his housemaid's son a reward with his own hands?

'The most revered person in our community, Nakulesh Chattopadhyay, is now presenting Palash with the prize!'

'Now the award is being handed over to Palash by Nakulesh Chattopadhyay, the most reverend person of our locality.' The entire premises is filled with clapping sounds.

Nakulesh *Babu* returns home at night. His face shows signs of exhaustion.

'What happened to you?' Mrs. Chattopadhyay ask to her husband.

'Kajol will not come to work from tomorrow.'

'Why? What's wrong?'

'It is my order.'

'But, simply explain to me why it is wrong? She is a good-hearted lady; she works admirably and furthermore she is also a trustworthy maid.'

"Regardless of how great she works or is faithful to us, she is the mother of Palash, to whom I have rewarded some time back. I hang my head in shame. The illiterate people of lower castes who we have long kept under our feet and who wouldn't dare speak in our presence are now... no... no...under any circumstances it can't be, Sraboni. You will hold Kajal back from coming to work from tomorrow. Her son Palash has occupied the place of our Tanmoy. It cannot be allowed. She should not cross the threshold of this house.'

****

11

The Inequality

Saddam Saikh

Phulia Sardar is sitting clumsily on the last seat of the class. The shade of the skin is blended dark. The eyes are small and swollen. Her appearance ends up being one of the particular listed individuals. Regardless of how early she arrives to class, she will be sitting on the back bench. They loathe, ridicule, and mistreat her because of her birth, most likely.

'Is it appropriate for you to study? You'd put some rice in your stomach by carrying bricks.' This is something Navina says to Phulia Sardar. The entire class bursts out laughing. She believes that by being admitted to this college, she has done a major sin. Phulia graduates with honours in Political Science from Muralidhar Girls College. The house is located in the village of Naliakhali. By bus, it takes two or three hours from Canning. She boards the bus at six a.m., carrying four loaves of bread and fried potatoes in a tiffin box. She cannot reach her first period on some days. But she doesn't expect even the most basic assistance from anyone.

Vijaya stands out among the other girls in the class. She takes a daring step that day, much to everyone's surprise.

'Come here, Phulia, and take a seat beside me.' Vijaya is in the second row of the bench. Phulia, perplexed, draws her apron more around her body and sits down. 'Don't you hear?' – Vijaya rushed up to her and immediately grabs her hand, telling her to go there – 'don't you hear?' Phulia's eyes well up with tears of fear.

'Leave me alone. I'm doing pretty well here.' Her eyes are filled with the urge of her plea. Vijaya turns a deaf ear to her. Vijaya grabs Phulia's hand and pulls her up to her bench, telling her to have a seat. Meanwhile, everyone was laughing and having a good time. But to everyone's surprise, Vijaya says – 'Listen. Phulia, you don't know me, even though we are in the same class. My name is Vijaya, Vijaya

Ganguly. You are my friend from today, do you understand my friend?' Like a charm, Phulia nods her neck in agreement.

Vijaya has a father and a mother and an elder brother. Her brother's name is Jeet. He graduates from Medical College last year and becomes a doctor.

Her father Amitabh Ganguly is an employee of a government office. They had spent so much time in a rented house in Jadavpur. They've been in Kasba for a few of months.

Mamata Ganguly has a master's degree in history. She works as a professor in a college in North Kolkata. Phulia's objections are not heard by Vijaya. She takes Phulia to their place one day. That day, mother does a little hard work that day. Water has to be used to clean the two-story stairwells and the chamber. She grumbles bitterly directing her wrath towards Vijaya. Of course, Vijaya isn't home at the time. She goes to Baliganj station to take the train to Phulia.

Going upstairs, Jeet notices his mother's activities and abruptly halts.

'Mom, what happened? Are you cleaning the stairs? Didn't Aunt show up for work?'

'Yes, she has arrived. She has returned after work. Don't you observe your sister's actions? She brought a Santhal from somewhere and said that the Santhal was her buddy. She placed her on the sofa after taking her to the second floor. Please refrain from sitting on the couch mattress since the fabric has not yet been drawn.'

'Why shouldn't I sit on the couch, mama? Why is it so? Moreover, doesn't she like us?' Without waiting for his mother's response, Jeet exits the house through the front door. Phulia has since made multiple visits to the Vijayas' home. Jeet and I have engaged in conversation and, over time, intimacy.

'Phulia, what do you think?'

'Do you think your society will accept me?'

'We cherish you, Phulia. The biggest truth is this. We adore human rights. Is there no truth to it?'

'Obviously, it isn't. But I'm scared. It is your mother, I fear. Will she consent?'

'Leave that up to me,' she said. Phulia's chest throbbed with tension as a deep breath escaped from within.

Jeet had to relocate to Medinipur Health Center in the meantime because of work. Jeet quickly earned the favour of the populace there. With complete honesty, he identified himself with their joy and grief. After five years there, he was forced to leave and return to Kolkata. Recently, he has joined Nilratan.

Phulia and Vijaya, meanwhile, earned their MAs and secured employment. Unlike Phulia, Vijaya was hired by a bank.

Phulia currently resides in a hostel for women in Kolkata. She vacations at home. Phulia resides with her parents, two older brothers, and younger brother Ratan Sardar, a student in the 12th grade. Both of the older brothers have jobs; one works for the railroad and the other works for the income tax office.

In awe, Vijaya peered at Phulia's home. She had no idea that the mud house could be so lovely. There are earthen walls everywhere. Thatch or hay is used to cover the upper portion of the house. Earth makes up the floor as well. Cow manure and soil are all over the house, rooms, veranda, and yard. Rice powder is spread across the floor and walls of the hunched-over house, looking like a painting on canvas. On the table, the bronze utensils from the porch are upside-down. They are sparkling in the sun's golden light. In one of the courtyard's corners, there are two ovens. Straw, mounds of cow manure, and jute sticks are used to decorate ovens. The oil has not yet been poured into an empty funnel on one side of the oven. On a mat in one corner of the yard, Paddy is drying. Rice is being scattered by four or five birds, who are chattering. A black-tailed dog appeared out of nowhere and sat down in the middle of the yard. It might be their pet.

Vijaya has never been to a village. She admires the beauty of the village with fascinated eyes. The village has changed. The moon's gentle light is no longer visible due to the lightning. The streets are illuminated by electricity. The village now hosts a market every day. The village is impacted by the city.

'Mom, I need to talk to you for a while, can you give me some time?'

Although Mamata Devi was a little taken aback by the way her son was speaking, she asked him to say whatever he wanted to say while keeping her thoughts as private as she could. 'I want to marry Phulia, mama,' Jeet replied without any doubt.

'Whom? How is that even possible? A Santhal girl, she is. They can be your buddies, but you can't wed them.

'But, Mom, I promised her.'

'You promised, right?' Mamata Devi mumbled something to herself. She stopped talking after grudgingly agreeing. Bhupen *Babu*, Mamata Devi's husband, passed away suddenly from a stroke a few years ago. She still isn't able to handle the shock.

They were married without a clarinet player and without conch. From the registry office Phulia went straight to her in-law's house as a daughter in-law. Mamata Devi agreed to the marriage but she was unable to forsake her caste and ethnicity. Therefore she wants to remind her at every step that she belongs to a lower caste.

'Dear Daughter-in-Law… hello Daughter-in-Law…'

Phulia rushed to the bathroom while busy. 'Why, mother?'

Vijaya already left the room by that point. Recent months have seen her marriage. Her husband Amitabh Banerjee is an engineer. They had a love marriage. Vijaya decided to visit Kasaba instead of going to work today so that she could spend time with Phulia. Instead of calling Phulia, her daughter-in-law, she addresses her by name.

'Daughter-in-law would you please check if the rice was cooked. If the water is dry, pour one mug of water; look dear – don't touch the pipkin. Lower the gas and walk away. I shall turn the pumpkin upside down.'

'What's wrong, Phulia? You washed the rice and put the pot on the oven. And now the rice is cooked and will you not be allowed to take the pumpkin down? Do you accept it?'

'Tell me, is there a way you may refuse to comply.'

'What's wrong, why all the shouting?'

'Okay, *Dada* Do you not observe anything? Is not Phulia being so affrontive?

'Affront? Who did it?'

'Why, mom? She doesn't allow Phulia to touch the pipkin. It's absolutely wrong not allowing Phulia to touch the rice, pupkin and even husk.'

Jeet left through the front door without responding.

'Mom, what kind of treatment is this with Phulia? She is a human like us, mom.' There was no benefit in Vijaya's words. The family adheres to its own set of rules.

Jeet had no intention of giving his son the sacred thread. It is a superstition in his opinion. It is the most effective method of dividing people from people. In the end, he was unable to refute his mother's assertions.

The house was filled with people that day. Phulia suddenly heard someone say in a mocking tone, 'Santal sons *Paite* ceremony?' The word was loudly said to Phulia intentionally.

That evening, Jeet and Phulia had a minor argument. When Phulia reached her extreme breaking point, she began acting irrationally and wandering about the home. Drops of sweat accumulated on her forehead even in the freezing weather of December.

****

12

The Woman

Tarik Anowar

The train is extremely crowded. But no one has sat on this side. Rita goes ahead a little and hears someone saying, 'don't go, don't go there…...the lunatic girl…. the lunatic girl'. Rita suddenly feels a little startled. She sees someone sitting awkwardly by the window. There is no one else around her. The seats are completely empty. Rita slowly moves forward and sits in the front seat. There is a sense of disgust in everyone's face.

Rita now looks at the woman. The woman has somehow covered herself with a tattered sari. Her age is around thirty. She rolls over her eyes strangely at everyone. Sometimes she mumbles alone. Rita recalls Anuradha *Baudi* who had left the house one midnight without informing anyone. After that, she never came back. Professionally Anuradha *Boudi* was a teacher. She was a benign, calm, affectionate woman, whose lips always had a sweet smile. But Anuradha *Boudi* one day changed drastically.

Ardhendu had just driven the car a little hastily. The pain in Anuradha was equally getting worse. Ardhendu had become nonplused. Seeing an older man in front of his car, he just took a turn to save the aged man but unfortunately, he lost his balance and ghastly collided the car with a light-post. Ardhendu became unconscious with the heavy jolt. As soon as he regained consciousness, he asked for Anuradha. Anuradha was then battling with death in the operation theater. She was bleeding heavily. She was given multiple bottles of blood. Then gradually, Anuradha brought back her consciousness and opened her eyes. The doctor too breathed a sigh of relief. He said – 'the patient is now out of danger so, there is no need to fear. But I'm sorry to tell you one thing that she can't be a mother anymore'. From then, Anuradha *Boudi* transformed into a different person. She had become silent and almost stopped talking. She was under psychological treatment for a few years. Ardhendu, all of a sudden, appeared at Rita's house with his long bushy beard and wearing a messy Punjabi clothe. There was a sign of sadness on his face. Rita was afraid of asking him anything. Yet she mustered courage and asked – 'Ardhendu, are you not well?'

Without answering that Ardhendu says – 'your *Boudi* has gone somewhere from the house last night. I searched for her everywhere but could not find her.' Ardhendu broke down into tears.

The woman gets up gently and walks towards the door – probably she will get off at the next station. Rita looks at her with unblinking eyes; the vision gradually becomes blurred; she explored the cast of Anuradha *Boudi* in the form of this woman. Slowly the image fades away; her reflection emerged on the sight of the woman's body.

****

13

The Virus

Saddam Saikh

The audience bursts into applause as Krishnendu ends his speech. He now gives excellent speeches. Krishnendu's speech is based on the belief that all humans are equal and that everyone has the right to live happily in this world. He has deeply entrenched himself in the minds and hearts of ordinary people in the village. He is a staunch supporter of the equality movement. In his face, he exudes a sense of knowledge. Krishnendu steps down from the platform and downs a glass of water. Atanu approaches him.

'Today, you have said it perfectly.' Krishnendu looks back. 'Where have you been for such a long time?' His lips curve into a smile.

'I went someplace. I've been here for quite some time. I have heard everything you said. It's quite nice. The debate, on the other hand, is Atanu's essence. All of the actual work has come to a halt. We have been unable to find a solution to the awful conditions in which Harijan was involved, as well as to the many other occurrences that have taken place since yesterday throughout Karnataka that we are not aware of. Have we ever been able to provide this with any specific solutions?'

'You have said exactly Krishnendu, how can that be remedied? Atanu takes a big breath and exhales it slowly. He keeps his cool and says that one day the door of consciousness for society's neglected people will be opened. And they will not die in that way. They will no longer be slave.'

'For this, revolution and struggle are required. However, some people have been awakened. They are fighting for the same rights as everyone else. It isn't just a problem in our country. The battle has started all around the world.' Krishnendu comes to a halt.

Atanu met Krishnendu at the house of Atanu's maternal uncle. Krishnendu is a friend of Atanu's cousin Subimal. At the time, they were both medical students. He visited Subimal's place frequently with his friend Subimal. Atanu was also a frequent visitor. That is how Krishnendu became acquainted with Atanu. Later on, the intimacy grew.

'Atanu, have you seen the village?'

'No, I haven't had much of an opportunity to visit the village.'

'Do you intend to visit the village?'

'Where?'

'In Burdwan, our home is there.'

'I will definitely go. Tell me when it's time to leave.'

'Tomorrow is the day.'

'Tomorrow? Okay, that's it.'

'Pack a little more winter clothes.'

'Now it is not so cold.'

'No, there is no less cold; it's bitterly cold there…'

The train stops at Burdwan station. They get down. The platform is packed with throngs of people. They push through the crowd and exit the station on their own.

'I didn't tell you Atanu that our home is 30 KM away from here. Then we'll have to walk another two miles to get to our destination.'

'What is there to say? Let me know on which side the bus will arrive, we need to board it.'

'The bus is usually stuck here. Unfortunately, we don't see any today. Let's enjoy a cup of tea together.'

The sound of the bus is only two feet away, and it feels like the bus has arrived. When Krishnendu sees the number, he replies, 'I don't think we can have tea anymore.' This is the bus we're on. A hefty luggage and a bag are being lugged around by Krishnendu. The same thing is happening to Atanu. The burden is a little too much for warm clothes.

Krishnendu disembarks the bus and takes a look around. He appears to be on the lookout for something? Rickshaws are sometimes accessible here, but not always. They go away for cultivation occasionally.

'Hey, do you have any problems walking? Please hand over the bag to me.'

'No, no, I'm fine, okay. You also have a suitcase and a bag.' There is a little passageway through the field. There are paddy farms on both sides. Nowadays, most countries follow the 12-month calendar. Burdwan is a great place for paddy farming. Everywhere the eyes go, all they see is green. Atanu was unaware of the beauty and variety of paddy fields. Sometimes, turmeric is scattered throughout a mustard field.

Atanu is in a nice mood. He'd seen paddy fields from afar while travelling by train, but he'd never seen them up close. Suddenly, he says in a cheerful tone,

'Sharpness of vision brings the vibration of life

Deep eyes search for your secret.'

'I had no idea you are a poet, Atanu.' Krishnendu is taken aback. Atanu grins.

The twilight passes us by as we walk along the trail. Krishnendu arrives and takes a position in front of a large home. This is where we call home. While driving down the road, Atanu didn't observe or catch a sight of any large structures. Almost every home is composed of mud, clay, tent straw, tile, or tin. As Atanu approaches the two-storey gate of Krishnendu's home, a boy of 18 years old steals the bag from him. She cast a shy glance his way. He gently instructs him to use the stairwell to go upstairs. As he ascends the stairs, he announces his intention to reside on the second floor, next to his elder brother's room.

There has been no electricity in any of the houses along the road. Krishnendu's home, on the other hand, is bathed in electric light. Krishnendu claims that on the journey, Atanu may not have noticed in the faint light that in the hamlet, the Panchayat system has been developed according to their wishes. Attempts to restore the half-buried electric poles along the roadside are nothing more than a ruse. With a simple smile, the electric light sometimes turns off. As a result, we've set up a generator to go with it. It only runs once in a while. Because you arrived today, the generator is turned on. In reality, under kerosene light, much of the time the entire town is in semi-darkness. 'Atanu, will you put water in your hand and mouth? Allow me to show you around the bathroom. – I'm going to wash my hands and face, as well as pour some water on my body.'

'In this frigid weather? Is there a need for hot water?'

'No, I'm going to take a cold bath.'

From the first floor, Mom's voice is heard. Hey, have you washed your hands and face? The *Luchi* is getting cold.

It's the middle of February. This time in Kolkata, there isn't even a smidgeon of cold. However, it is really cold here. Atanu is dressed in a long-sleeved sweater. Even so, the cold isn't going away for him. At night, it was more frigid.

Atanu and Krishnendu descend the stairwell. Both of them head out to the paddy field after eating breakfast. They continue down the paddy field's edge.

'Atanu, have a look to that side. Our mango orchard is all that can be seen. Later, I'll take you there. We have a large lake. Can you swim?'

'Yes, I learned something.'

'What do you think about taking a dip in the lake?'

Krishnendu is on his way to the village now. The road is extremely congested. During the rainy season, there must be a lot of muddy water on the roads. The hamlet residents' misery knows no bounds.

Krishnendu believes that this is the state of most of the villages since he understands Atanu's mind. During the rainy season, the ground becomes quite muddy. Seeing the village, Atanu thinks that very ordinary persons living here. Those people who comes under below poverty level. All are mud houses here. Houses were made of either straw or tent. Houses were made of either straw or tent.

Atanu observes the village and concludes that it is populated by fairly ordinary people who are on the verge of becoming impoverished. Here, most of the houses are made of mud with roof made of reeds or tarpaulins.

Krishnendu come to a halt in front of a home. – 'Aunt, aunt…' Krishnendu calls out clearing his throat. From inside, a voice asks, 'Who are you?'

'My name is Krishnendu'

'Krishnendu, come, come inside the room.'

'No, no I'm sitting here at veranda.'

'Lavoni, my dear mom; please spread a mat on the veranda.' A fifteen or sixteen-year-old girl approaches with a mat in her hands.

Aunty takes the mat from her hands and tells that Satyen has been suffering from a high fever for a few days and that her mind is not in a pleasant mood.

'Have you given him any medications?'

'Yes. I'm just giving him the same water that Gurudev brought yesterday. I've saved the bowl of water he used to bathe his feet. I gave him some water to drink.

'Aunty, what did you do? You offered him foot-washing water.'

'Let me check on Satyen.'

He's lying on a mat on that house's veranda. He's currently suffering from a high fever. He was just raving about a few minutes ago. Let's see what happens. Lavoni lifts the *kantha.*

Satyen has his eyes closed. The sound of moaning fills the room. Krishnendu take a few steps forward. He keeps his hands on his brow. 'Oh, my God! The body is sweltering from a fever. It is necessary to provide water. Did you put water on his head, Auntie?'

'He will catch cold so I did not give him water. Moreover, *Gurudev* told him to drink his recited water. And he said that he would get better with that.'

'You people have made the mistake aunty, providing water to the head during a fever does not make it cool; it only helps lessen the fever. The patient seemed to be at ease. Make arrangements to water Satyen's head.'

Lavoni gets a pail of water and pours it over Satyen's head with a kettle.

'Aunty, I'm giving you a prescription; please carry it with you.'

'All right, *Baba*.'

'I'll return tomorrow to see how Satyen is doing. Let's get started, Atanu.' Aunty always remembers to give him his medicine on time. Don't think too much about it. There's no need to be concerned. While crossing the yard, Krishnendu says these words. He looks at his wristwatch. Above the head, the sun is angled to the west… It's already 2.00 a.m. 'Since the morning, I haven't had anything in my stomach. Hunger appears to cause the stomach's intestines to be digested.'

'Atanu, do you want something to eat?'

'Yes, I'm getting to get hungry. It's said in quiet tones by Atanu. The mother emerges as soon as the gate opens. And you both left the house in the morning, and then I did not hear anything of you since. Do you realise you didn't feed him for the entire day? What will his reaction be?'

'No, no aunty, you please don't think anything' – she says with a timid tone.

'Mom, we're now taking a bath. You continue to pour rice onto the plate.' Krishnendu holds Atanu's hand and walked up the second-floor staircase.

Yesterday's incident is a new experience for Atanu. It is as if he had previously heard the story from his mother and grandmother. Atanu never imagined he'd be experiencing such events on the eve of the new millennium. Wherever people dream of living on the world, the village's poorest residents are still tricked in the same way.

The two of them are walking side by side silently.

Two males were passing by at the time, conversing. '*Gurudev* is a good physician, but his medicine didn't work either,' one says to the other. Satyen is knocked out. 'Isn't there a devil inside him?'

Krishnendu gives them a gentle glance as soon as their words reach his ears. 'Have you listened to what they've said?' Atanu speaks in hushed tones.

Krishnendu approaches them and asks, 'Do you come from Satyen's house? How is he doing these days?'

'He's not very good. He then turns to Krishnendu and asks, 'Are you Krishnendu?'

'Yes.'

'When have you come from Kolkata?'

'It's been two or three days.'

'Who is with you? I couldn't recognise him.'

'Atanu, my friend.'

'Are you going to Satyen's home?'

'Yes.'

'Go, go hurriedly. You will diagnose Satyen. You are a physician. They rush over to Satyen's home.'

'Why is it so crowded? You all move a little. Make his head space a little more open. Aunty, how is Satyen doing these days?'

'He isn't doing good, *Baba*. Since last night he has been suffering from loose motion.'

'Ouch.' Krishnendu leans in close to Satyen's body. There isn't any reaction. Krishnendu gets the injection ready. Please, Atanu, raise Satyen's hand a little higher. Someone was going to place *prasadi* flowers on Satyen's head and a tablespoon of water in his mouth in the meantime.

'No, no don't give that water in his mouth.'

'Why should I not give?' The woman is taken aback by Krishnendu's appearance. It's not just water, she claims, but Shitala Mother Temple's *Charanamrit*. Satyen will get better if he consumes it.'

'All right, you may take it elsewhere or toss it out. They're poisonous, and that's not a good thing.'

'Ok, you can take it somewhere else or throw it away. They are toxic, not good.'

'We've been treated with these things our entire lives, and you tell us to throw them away!' Krishnendu instructs aunty to give Satyen boiling water without paying heed. He still hasn't regained consciousness. Krishnendu seemed to be a little worried. He keeps glancing at his wrist watch after the injection and a dark shadow on his face become thicker and larger. Satyen's wife enterers the room and sits next to him. His eyes are partially closed, as if he wants to make a gesture.

'Maybe he'll take a drink of water. Fill his mouth with two teaspoons of the boiling water.' Satyen's wife pours a spoonful of water into her husband's mouth. She wipes his face with her apron as some water spills down his cheeks. Now, Krishnendu seems to be a little calm.

'Aunty, I brought these pills, but some more pills are required. You can request someone to buy it. There's no need to worry; he'll bounce back shortly.' This time, Krishnendu turns to Atanu and says, 'Let's go. Today I'm going swimming at the pond. My head is a little bit achy. Despite how far science has come, people are still in that basic stage. Atanu, do you get that?'

Atanu adds that some persons have been detained in this state for a long period. 'However, Atanu, I think that their current predicament is the result of their own shortcomings.'

'Yes, their intellect is to blame, but it is not a cunning intellect.'

This word was too much for Krishnendu to take in. 'I'll talk to you about it later,' he says. Let's go swimming in the pond now.' They sink and float in the crystal clear water as they walk down the stairs step by step.

Previously, the locals drank the water from this pond. The government has installed water taps throughout the streets. As a result, everyone now bathes, washes, and cleans their clothes only here. After dinner, he was getting ready to sleep. Drowsiness has overflowed on his eyes right now. Atanu's sleep is abruptly interrupted by the sound of a garbled voice. Krishnendu isn't by his side. Atanu gets out of bed and sits up.

'They will follow my rules; do you get it, Krishnendu?'Atanu raises his ears. The words are hardly audible, yet they are clear.

'You can't cheat on them like that anymore, dad. Why did you return to Satyen's place the other day? You were forbidden by me, father.'

'Wouldn't I go if you didn't want me to?'

'No, you won't be able to. Why did you tell them they couldn't take the medicine I gave them?'

'You also prohibited them from consuming recited water.'

'Yes, I prohibited them from doing so since it is harmful.'

'Look, Krishnendu, that's what they're used to.'

'Did you know that Satyen's stomach ailment worsened after he drank the water used to wash your feet? It was conceivable that he would pass away.'

'What would have occurred if that had happened? They have always perished in this manner.'

'I'm telling you, dad, don't torture them like this any longer.'

'I know what to do and what not to do. You don't have to be a genius.'

'You must take it if necessary. I can't allow you continue doing what you've been doing for so long. Dad, I'm a doctor.'

'You travel to Kolkata and teach all of these lessons. Even if you aren't dealing with them, it's not a problem.' Then he whispered, 'It's too late now, go to sleep,' in a quiet voice.

This conversation is no longer extended by Krishnendu. Slowly, he makes his way to his own room. As he tries to close the door, he makes a small noise. He sits next to Atanu and rests his head on the cushion. He slips into a deep slumber in an instant. Atanu, on the other hand, do not sleep. For so long, he was sleeping calmly with his head on the pillow. He gets up and sits on the bed this time. He has seen Krishnendu in squint eyes. He gets out of the bed. Taking the water from the table he gulps it down through his throat. He has seen Krishnendu in squint eyes. The night is becoming increasingly dark and ominous. The profound darkness around is deafeningly silent. Atanu lights a cigarette from a packet of cigarettes he had in his shirt pocket. He stands on the veranda after softly unlocking the door.

Outside, it is pitch black, but he notices a weird light. He is enchanted by the shadow of darkness. A black owl flies through the window and perches on the cornice. It wings its way again. This world has never stopped being diverse. He takes another drag from his cigarette. As he enters the room, he pours some water into his mouth once more. The throat is becoming increasingly dry. That melody keeps echoing in his head – 'it's not right dad to deceive people in this way.'

'What is cheating according to you? Our grandfather and father own this business. This is how I was able to prepare you for your current position as a doctor. All of the lands, all of the money, everything...' Taking a little pause, he says that 'if they gain greater intellect, our happiness will be jeopardised. Our capital is their idiocy.'

Atanu feels tingle in his head. He is in excruciating pain. The sky gradually becomes brighter in the morning. The cries of crows can be heard in the distance from the branches of a tree. Atanu walks down the stairs. With the gate in hand, he walks out the door. Then he takes a walk down the street. The two dogs started barking at each other. He tries to calm the dogs with his gentle touch. The fog has engulfed the entire area. As a result, everything is invisible. He goes onward, pushing the fog behind him. Eventually, the preoccupation of the fog will be broken by the daylight...

****

14

The Lover's Death

Tarik Anowar

The year is 1971. In all of East Bengal, a liberation battle has begun. In order to liberate Bengal from Pakistan's rule, the East Bengal forces have protested against brutality. Under the government of Pakistan, they have been completely disturbed in every way. Pakistan, though, seems unwilling to let them go easy. Cities and villages are on fire from conflict and bloodshed. The East Bengali people are the victims of inhumane acts committed by the Pakistani army. They are using machine guns to shoot everybody in their path. It appears as though East Bengal as a whole has been turned into a battlefield. Fighting turned furious among the freedom forces. The enormous exodus crosses the India-Pakistan border into India out of fear for their life. Tragically, thousands of civilians have died at the hands of the Pakistani military. Indira Gandhi, the prime minister of India, has extended a helping hand to the refugees. Several locations have been designated as refugee camps. Indian volunteers are still giving their all to help them. Salt Lake has also established a camp for refugees. It was built using soil from the Ganges River. The area is still heavily covered in enormous Hogla trees.

Subimal has been working nonstop since the morning. He now knows that around a month ago, Neela's family left East Bengal and sought refuge in the Salk-Lake refugee camp. He is really anxious about this information. He whistles while singing the autumnal lullaby. A hidden romantic feeling thrills his heart. Does Neela still feel the same way about him? Or has she totally forgotten about him? What does she now look like? She must have been more beautiful.

Subimal resided in a hostel while studying at Bagerhat. Over the holidays, he used to visit his family. Neela would have been counting down the days till his arrival. Compared to Subimal, Neela was a few years younger. They had been friends since they were young. In Subimal's home, there was a flower garden full with a variety of colourful flowers, including Jasmine, Malati, Gardenia, Kanthali-

Champa, and Bel. Neela used to visit their garden every morning to collect flowers. Subimal assisted her in gathering the flowers.

As soon as a recollection popped into Subimal's head, a smile broke out on his face.

'Will you be my wife, Neela?'

'What do you say?'

'Why not? When we grow up, we will get married.' Neela runs away, flapping her two braids in embarrassment.

Subimal won't return home during this Puja holiday. His school's final exam is coming up soon. He therefore has no intention of wasting any time this year. He notified Neela of this. However, Subimal was unable to control himself till the test. He returns home because of Neela's powerful magnetic pull of love. Neela is Subimal's junior in class academically. Neela has gone to her uncle's house, which Subimal discovers when he gets back home. She intends to stay a few days. Their home is far from her uncle's home. It is almost five miles away. You have to travel either on foot or by water. Subimal sets out his journey. He spotted black clouds forming in the northwest sky after a while of strolling. Subimal was almost blown away by a wind gust. The flowing dust in the storm started to hit his face with great force. The orchards of jackfruit and mango are about to perish. Just near his ear, a blackberry tree branch drops to the ground. In fright, Subimal retreats two paces. Then the clouds roared and there was a flash of lightning. Then the torrential rain begins to fall. It appears that the icy darkness of midnight is outside at twelve o'clock in the afternoon. Additionally, the birds flee to their nests. On the tree branches, their chirp may be heard. Two wet crows are licking each other's beaks while perched on a mango branch. They might be splitting a little amount of the meal. The heavy rain has made the muddy road extremely slick. When Subimal was ready to fall, he clutched a tree stump. He controls himself in some way. There is no indication that there are any people nearby. A bolt of lightning strikes abruptly and loudly. A burning coconut tree is discovered by Subimal. The wrath of nature terrifies him. He still has a ways to go. Subimal has only been able to travel halfway thus far. Immediately after the thunderstorm passed, severe rain started to fall. Subimal is thoroughly drenched in the rain. His moist body is making him feel chilled. If there was a small shelter somewhere, that would be good. Right now, Subimal was unable to determine the location of

Neela's uncle's home. Only once, many years ago, did he come here with Neela's parents. It was pouring cats and dogs in the meantime. He remembers that there was a huge Banyan tree on the path leading up to Neela's uncle's front door. Subimal makes a little more progress on his walk. Bijon, the youngest uncle of Neela, is waiting at the front entrance. He appears to be almost Subimal's age. In the village school, they used to be in the same class. Bijon used to travel by boat to school.

'Hey, Subimal, you're right here.' He appears astonished as he turns to face Subimal.

'Yeah, just arrived.'

'You are wet from head to toe. Hold on while I get the towel and use it to wipe your head first.'

'I need to wash my legs because they are covered in mud.'

'Wait, let me get the umbrella; we're going to the pond,' he said. Subimal's visit to their home is well known to Bijon. Even he inquires, 'Subimal, what brings you here?'

'Has Neela arrived?'

'Yeah. But why do you need her?'

'There's a demand. Will you give her a call?'

'But you can not to meet her today?'

'Why?'

'Her wedding date will be decided upon today.'

'Her prospective in-laws' guests have arrived. How is she going to meet you now?'

'Please go and let her know I'm coming; Neela will definitely be there.' Bijon quickly enters to make a call to her. Neela isn't prepared to meet him though. Neela puts a ring given by Subimal in her uncle's hand and says, 'please give it to him and this letter as well.'

Now there is no rain. The sun is visible in the sky. No one can now tell that the sky was previously so erratic. There is brilliant sunlight everywhere. Subimal unfolds the letter.

Subimal,

I am giving you the ring back. In a month, I will be getting married. You are invited. Kindly come.

Thank you
Neela.

Subimal apprehends a tinge of irritation in his eyes. While he is unconscious, a tear escapes his eyes and falls to the ground. The idea of that day greatly disturbs his heart. His heart is very agitated by the thought of that day.

They walked up to the river side. The river's tidal waters appear to be overflowing right now. The fishermen are off in the middle of the river, fishing from a boat.

Neela and Subimal are seated next to one other. Subimal tenderly clasps Neela's one hand in his own. He then releases the ring's knot and places it on Neela's finger.

'What are you doing?'

'From today you are only mine.'

Then they enjoyed the serene atmosphere sitting on the river bank for a long time. The light of the day begins to fade away. The sun in the sky sets down on the far side of the river. It seems as if someone is smearing the red colour on the western horizon. Two white-coloured ospreys flew to that horizon and then disappeared in the sky. They are gradually suffused by soft dense darkness of the evening. They look at each other spellbound. Then the moment appears when Subimal says – 'now it is evening and we have to bid farewell.' Subimal enjoys the peeping of the moon through gap of the trees. Neela, it is quite cold at the beginning of this winter.

'Yeah, it is cold enough.'

'Subimal, when will you come again?'

'In the summer vacation.'

'Subimal, a girl is looking for you.'

'Where is she, Joyanta?'

'Come with me. She is waiting there.' Neela was standing there. Looking at Subimal, she moves forward.

'Neela you are here, what is the matter?'

'Yeah, I could not help coming here.'

'Why Neela, is there any bad news?'

'Yes Subimal. My parents have made the decision regarding my marriage. I informed them that I would not get married right away.

However, they are determined in their choice. Subimal, what should I do right now?'

Subimal doesn't say anything for a time. 'What should I do now, Neela?' he responds. All over his face, the frozen, dark clouds are pervasive.

I can't think of anyone else but you, Subimal.

But Neela, I'm at a loss for words right now. My school's final exam is coming up. Please persuade your parents to hold off for a few years.

Despite having high expectations for Subimal, Neela refuses to speak. Neela's eyes began to tear up. With a handkerchief, Subimal dabbed her eyes. Neela maintains a downcast expression.

'What will happen next, Subimal?' With a broken voice and wet eyes, Neela asks.

'Neela, I am not in a position to marry you at this time.' Subimal has trouble falling asleep because of this problem. He is unable to reach a sound judgement. He believed he wouldn't return home before the test. But a mysterious and powerful attraction lured him back. In fear, Subimal repeatedly rolls the ring between his fingers.

Indistinctly his lips pronounce her name, 'Neela….'

Neela has finally arrived in Salt Lake after so many years. Since the morning, Subimal has felt a little disoriented. He exhibits a funny demeanour, which Anjana has long noticed.

'Tell me what happened to you, please. You have seemed irrational since the morning.' With his work bag, a handkerchief, and a glass of water in her hand, Anjana approaches Subimal. Subimal pretends not to hear her. He takes the bag and hankie from his wife and sips some water from the glass. 'Anjana, I have some works today, so it will be a little late to get home,' he explains as he delivers the glass to her. Shovan needs my assistance with the shopping because his sister is getting married soon.

Anjana carries Toban on her lap as she advances toward the gate. Two years ago, they tied the knot. In less than a year, Anjana became pregnant, preventing them from taking their honeymoon.

'I never had the chance to travel anywhere pleasantly after the marriage because of you. You're a lucky lady, Anjana. Tell me how many individuals receive this chance.' He then breaks out in laughter.

'Listen, Toban has grow up now. How will it be if we leave him with my mother while we go on our honeymoon? He no loger takes my breast milk. In addition, I also have a younger sister. She looks after Toban well. Now let's take a trip to Shillong.'

'Okay, dear, your request will be met.'

They must first take a bus from the Dumdum airport to Guwahati before continuing on to Shillong. Anjana has never taken a flight before, although Subimal has undoubtedly done so on occasion for work-related reasons. At 1.25 PM, the jet is supposed to take off. Anjana is highly interested about the trip. By using a taxi, Subimal and Anjana arrived at the airport in plenty of time to board the plane. With their hands folded, the air hostesses greet the passengers as they enter the aircraft. They proceed and place themselves at the reserved seats. Before the plane takes off, they buckle their seat belts as ordered by the airhostess.

The plane twitches at first before accelerating along the runway. They experience a sharp shock before continuing to soar above the sky. Anjana scans the view out the window. The blue-colored clouds are drifting around the black clouds in space, which resemble mountains. Anjana is utterly enthralled by the scenes.

The chocolate is delivered on a platter by the Airhostess. She grasps one with one finger, pulls out the piece of paper, and then puts it in her mouth. They eventually receive lunch. While eating, Anjana looks out the window. This time, the image gradually fills in with the earth's vegetation and dwellings.

'Anjana, the plane is about to land.'

'Subimal, we have reached Guwahati so early, I suppose? Just take a look outside.'

The vacation had been exceedingly enjoyable for Subimal and Anjana, even amid the bitter cold of Shillong.

Subimal moved to India that year with his mother, brother, and sisters after taking his last test at school. Even though he knew she was married, he used to miss her terribly during the early stages of their relocation. All of those recollections gradually vanished as time went on. However, today all of a sudden those memories have come to life once more. Even Subimal cannot comprehend the rationale. He struggles to focus on his office tasks.

He sets out for Salt Lake in the afternoon. The distance from Ultodanga to Salt Lake is quite longer and the only way is on foot.

There is nothing but desert and sand dunes as far as the eye can see. Subimal had no choice but to begin moving. Neela has taken refuge somewhere in the Salt Lake Refugee Camp, but Subimal is unaware of this. Without knowing the block number, it is incredibly challenging to locate her.

He still moves toward Salt Lake in spite of all of these obstacles.

When Subimal reaches Salt Lake, he appears to be lost. Who will let him know where Neela has sought safety? Subimal's mind appears to be blank thinking about what to do. He moves around like a nomad, going here and there.

'Are not you Subimal?' The sound that shouted out his name astonished Subimal. He has startled eyes as he observes the stranger.

'Oho! Do you not recognise me, I'm Bijon? Do you still recall Neela? I am Bijon, her uncle.'

Subimal experiences some shame. He ought to have known who Bijon was. Bijon approaches and extends his hand to him.

'Follow me, Neela has come. They've arrived. You want to meet her, right?'

'Yeah.' He responds in a broken tone.

'Then follow me,' he said.

'Neela, take a look at who I brought here.' Neela arrives and approaches him. Subimal first struggles to believe what he is seeing. Neela is dressed in a standard sari. On her lap was a five-year-old boy who was crying for something. Neela slaps him on the cheek after failing to meet his demand. From his mother's lap, the wailing infant drops to the ground. A boy of ten-or twelve-years old approaches Subimal and takes a seat next to him.

'He is your uncle, therefore touch his feet.'

'No, no, it's alright.' Subimal regains control of his legs.

Subimal simply stares at Neela.

– Who is this woman? Is this the same Neela he previously fell in love with? She is not Neela, not at all. Neela has not left even the slightest trace on her body. Her eyes are not as appealing as Neela's. Below her eyes, there are black blotches. She also appeared to have lost her vision. Her condition has deteriorated. It appears as though Subimal is unable to compare this Neela to his familiar Neela. He senses some type of void in his heart. He uses his handkerchief to dab away his sweat. The wide open area in front of him is deserted, uninhabited, and covered with white sand dunes.

****

15

The Special Maid

Saddam Saikh

The train has arrived at the station. It is a winter's morning, that's why the darkness of night has not still gone away. In the fog, Kolkata has wrapped itself in a strange image of dawn. Ketoki covers her body well with the edge of her garment. Then she also gets off the train with many others. Crowds of people have gathered in the station premises. Everyone is running in pursuit of livelihood and in the hope of survival. At the end of the day's work whatever is earned is taken home binding in the border of the cloth. This is how life goes on. They have become robots by listening to the rude words of Memsahib. The competition of who can earn more money goes on from one flat to another flat. Ketoki stands in front of the door. She knocks on the door. But there's no response. Once again, she rattles the latch of the door. This time Ketoki puts his hand on the calling bell. She has been forbidden to press the calling bell. Sleep is disturbed in the morning. Now the sound comes from another side – 'who?'

'I – I am Ketoki.' Now the door is open. The gentlewoman tells her in a slight angry voice – 'why have you not come for four days?' Ketoki hesitantly says 'My child was down with fever'. 'You all always get ill. Today you fall sick, tomorrow your son will fall sick and the day after tomorrow someone else will fall sick. There's is nothing to do but lie; this is the habit of low caste people. I have kept another one. Now you have come.' The door is closed on her face. Tears roll down her face. She wonders why she is born in a low caste family. Otherwise, she would not have had to listen to this harsh word. She remembers her son very badly. Her son has been suffering from fever for a few days and has become very weak. Yesterday she boiled a little amount of papaya and fed him with rice. Her whole body shivers thinking about the pathetic situation of her son. In the darkness of dawn at the end of the night the child is deprived of the warmth of the edge of his cloth. That darkness is taking him from one door to another. She is in a helpless situation. There is no one else in her life except that only boy. After one year of marriage, she had to return to her father's house. Pocha was born eight months later. So, she did not have a place in his father-in-law's house. With false accusations in her head, she was forced to say goodbye to her father-in-law's house by holding her one-day-old son in her arms. The family members of her father-in-law beat her out of the house. They didn't hear anything of Ketoki.

Pocha needs to learn; he needs to be a nice human being like others. She has tremendous ambitions concerning Pocha's future. A few days ago, Ketoki traveled to the metropolis, abandoning her village. They took shelter in a Jhuggi. She has already enrolled Pocha in a school. With the assistance of the street light, he is continuing his studies. Illiterate Ketoki is never short of conscience. Ketoki understands what blindness is. She doesn't want Pocha to be blind; she will make him study, make him a man.

Pocha leaves for school and returns. He does really well in school. All of his grades were superb. He's the only one of his kind in the whole class. But somehow, there is a huge difference between him and the rest of the others. With the name *Pocha* which literally means rotten in Bengali, his friends harass him, calling *Alu Pocha*, *Begun Pocha*; he burst into tears while saying all that to his mother. His mother promises him that everything will be alright while rubbing the tears – 'one day, when you learn a lot, when you secure a job, they will tell you nothing.' Pocha stopped weeping and glanced at his mother; mom is telling me the truth. A sigh of relief came out from the little chest and was released into the air.

That day, they call Pocha at the tiffin to play. Pocha didn't want to play; instead, he intended to sit in the library and read. As the test exam was going to approach, he thought to refrain from playing.

'You know Biplab; it seems Pocha doesn't want to play.'

'Why not? Pocha has to be a Doctor or Engenieer in future. Isn't it Pocha?'

Pocha doesn't answer. Rather he gets irritated. Noticing that Pallab further says that, 'you know Biplab, those who qualify Joint Entrance in reservation quota and become doctor, they only kill people.' Biplab reacts to this in mop and mow.

'Why? Does the examination consider only reservation? They have to qualify it right – equally among others.' Now Pocha answers to this.

'See the dumb start talking genius? You people are insulting your ancestors by not going to plough in the field. Do we deny our ancestors' job?' Meanwhile he shows his sacred thread. 'Now I must tell how you have learnt is more than enough for you. Now go and start ploughing in the countryside.' All starts laughing at him.

At that moment Pocha reminds the word of Haran. 'Study is not our cup of tea, Pocha. Education is the matter of gentlemen. You know that they mock us calling our caste name. And they laugh at us. I find all of these to be completely intolerable. I won't ever return to school'

'Look, Haran – if we don't go to school like this and if we don't study then their purpose will be fulfilled. That's what they want, Haran.' Haran thinks Pocha's words as very reasonable. He says in a calm voice that 'Pocha, you have opened my eyes and ears.'

At this moment he thinks of his village. He thinks of his aunt named *Bamun*. He remembers the memory of the whole village he has forgotten for so long. The deep story of that day is still clear in one corner of the memory.

'Oh shit, you have touched the bank; you have spoiled the water of my earthen pitcher!' Angered, she poured water from the jar into the bank. The water rolls and merges into the pond again.

'Aunt, I have not touched your earthen pitcher.'

'You have not touched the pot but you have touched the bank of pond.'

Pocha does not make out how water of the earthen pot gets wasted without touching it. Despite that he repeatedly swims to the bank and touches it out of curiosity. He was pouring down water of the earthen pot of his aunt; *Bamun* was on the bank of pond. This time she walks towards Pocha's house with empty jug without water.

Pocha's restless body then danced in the rhythm of the water. Two ducks were quacking in the water and the sound was reverberating in the pond. Pocha was also swimming to their beat. A kingfisher bird picks up a fish with its beak and sits on a tree; the fish is picked up by the bird in such a way that it appears to be floating in mid-air like a fool. Pocha is unaware when he has come on the bank of the pond and is swinging his legs back and forth. The water of the head has dried up without a towel. Suddenly, with a cold touch in his ear, he returns from the world of absent-mindedness. 'Why didn't you let *Bamun* Didi take water?' Grandmother grabs his ear and makes him stand up. 'Why don't I let her take water? She herself did not take water.' 'You do injustice and say big words in your mouth; they are our respected elders, our goddess; if they touch us their position falls in danger and we also do sin. After death we have to go to hell and suffer punishment.'

He was unable to distinguish that day between the thoughts of the illiterate people of that village and the educated individuals of the city. The chest wants to sigh for a long time but is suppressed, leaving it empty. The final school exam is approaching. Now, Pocha is being looked after at school very well.

But it doesn't have any effect on him. He knows where their weakness is; why they want to suppress everyone. Everyone notices his energetic attitude. Inwardly they are scared of him. His straight forward words sometimes pierce at them. Ketoki is getting older thereby she can't work hard like before. Yet she works hard for her son. Nowadays Pocha serves as a tuition teacher in two or four places; he forbids his mother to do more work now. But she doesn't listen. Now she cooks in two or three houses. Therefore, she gets a little bit more money and works much less. But Ketoki is in need of money. She wipes her forehead with the edge of her cloth. Now her hard work has been worthwhile. Pocha has passed M. A. He needs a job now. He prefers teaching at school. But it's not easy to be a government teacher, although he has good academic scores. Ketoki can't wait anymore. This time she wants to start a family with her son's marriage. That's why she doesn't want to wait even for one day.

'Mother, why are you getting so restless? Look, mother, I will manage at least something.' He did not have to wait so long. Pocha got a job in a high school in South Kolkata. Finally, Ketoki's dream is going to be fulfilled. But Pocha did not realise that this would start a new chapter in his life. From the very first day he is not allowed to sit in the teacher's room at school. He is not even allowed to take classes. His classes are being taken with the staff of class four. Occasionally, sports classes are given to this short black man. And his water supply system is not with the other teachers. He has to drink water from outside with the other boys. Pocha is the only SC teacher in this school. As it continued for long time Pocha felt suffocated there, he claims his rights. His salary was stopped. Pocha alone was confident to counter them. In this situation, he approached to the law, but he was emotionally broken as he didn't get proper justice there. Then one day he was badly thrashed as soon as he entered through the school gate. When Pocha realised they were indeed his students, he was shocked. Later it was revealed that a strange warrant had been issued against him. Pocha is a homosexual. Tormented with shame and humiliation, Pocha almost got mad.

Ketaki feels a strange pain in her head. The sleeping crabs began to bite and bite into her head innumerable times. Ketaki abruptly become enraged. This uneducated woman has noticed fire diffraction that is unprecedented. Her eyes began to flicker with the flare of fire. In utter rage, she squeezed her right hand into a fist. Holding Pochar's hand with her left hand, she says – 'Time is beckoning us; don't delay more…'

****

16

Accident

Tarik Anowar

Shyamal does not feel up to having sleep at all. He flips and tosses around while lying on the bed. Trishna is sleeping soundly. Her one hand touches Tumpa's body. Tumpa budges a little in her sleep. She puts her hand around her mother's neck. Shyamal leaves the office today a bit early and comes home. His health condition is well. However, there is slight fever in his body. To avoid disturbing their slumber, Shyamal climbs out of bed as quietly as a mouse. In the darkness, he walks forward to the table and switches on the lamp. To keep his throat moist, he pours a little water to the glass and sips it. Now his thirst has been quenched. Sitting on a chair, he is about to light a cigarette. In the meantime, his phone suddenly starts ringing. He is a bit startled by the sound of someone's phone at late night. He picks up the phone, thinks for a moment and then holds it to his ear. He hears the voice of Moloy from the other side of the phone.

'What do you say, accident?'

'When?'

The Darjeeling mail collided head-on with Habra local train in the evening. Many people were injured and the death toll is quite high.

'What do you say, Purnendu is now in Hospital?'

'Which hospital?'

'R.G. Kour'

'Yes, all right, I'm coming to your house in the early morning. You will be ready for that.' Then Shyamal puts down the receiver. He looks very anxious.

'Whose phone was it?'

Shyamal fails to heed Trishna calling. Last evening, he had a talk with Purnendu. They left the office together. Shyamal had some work in Borobzaar [Bigmarket], so he parted from Purnendu on the way. Shyamal couldn't realise that their separation was forever. He did not observe when Trishna came and stood beside him.

Many dead bodies are wrapped in white clothes in the hospital. A large crowd gathers around it. Everyone seems to be lost in bemoaning the sudden death of their kinsman. Today, the entire hospital premises are like a rush of mourning people. Shyamal continues to move forward on his slow legs. Purnendu is now in eternal sleep. His body is no longer energetic today, it is now a corpse. Just a few hours ago, it was a human body. Tears appear in Shyamal's eyes. Sitting next to Purnendu's body, his wife is crying covering her face with the end of her sari. Gradually they go ahead.

'Shyamal *Da*?'

Shyamal looks flabbergastingly at Dibendu's call.

'Dibendu, you?'

'Yes, Shyamal *Da*. I have also brought *Boudi* with me.'

'Then who is she?'

'We are in great trouble; they are not giving us the dead body.'

'Why?'

'Look at the woman crying in the hospital premises. Two unknown men have brought her dressed up as *Dada's* wife. A lawyer is also with them. They don't even allow us to go near the corpse.'

'What? How is it possible?' There is question and confusion in Moloy's eyes.

With great astonishment in his eyes, Dibendu says, 'the government has also offered condolence over this accident.' The government has agreed to compensate the affected families financially in some way. Many bodies have been removed and some have also been taken over in this declaration. They are also squatters like those.

The afternoon turned into night in search of the body that day. The woman could not become successful in acting as fake wife. Purnendu's wife Aparna is standing a little away. Her eyes are almost dried up from the suddenness of the incident. She has become dumb after crying heart-breakingly. By then, all the kith and kin of Purnendu have arrived. The unidentified actors who made false claims have since vanished from the place.

It is almost 12 o'clock at night. Purnendu's body is taken to the Lorry. The hospital premises suddenly shakes with a loud noise. The entire atmosphere is overcastby the deep dark smoke.

****

17

The Yolk

Saddam Saikh

It's eerily silent everywhere. It has poured heavily a little while ago. A bitterly cold evening has descended. Rain has made it frigid to the bone. The road becomes desolate. A few rickshaws keep making futile attempts to shatter the silence.

In the light of the lamp post, Akash glances at the clock. It's only 8.30 at night; so it's not much. Meanwhile, the thick night's darkness has engulfed half of the city. Akash moves a little more quickly. A shadow emerges in front of him out of the darkness. He was a little shocked. Now the shadow speaks – 'aren't you Akash?' He stared Renu in the eyes as he raised his head. His face was flushed with surprise.

'Hey, Renu?'

The impression in Akash is as if the sky has extended far and wide via the eardrums on the screen of the picture that floats from the depths of the mind, which goes by playing a mournful tune by manipulating the strings of Setar.

'I wasn't expecting to see you in this condition... So you're a little taken aback?'

Akash is taken aback when he learns that Renu has married an engineer. They have relocated to Delhi. He'll meet her in this way, he did not anticipate that.

Renu adds, chuckling, 'Akash, life is truly variegated like a river.' It is a forming and breaking activity.

Renu has lost a lot of weight. At such age he has started wearing eyeglasses. Green is her favourite colour. She can still easily recognise the green. Isn't that lovely smile on the corner of her lips still there? She is dressed in a green saree. Akash was completely unaware of the situation because it was so dark.

'Why are you silent, Akash?'

'Thinking…'

'What are you thinking?'

'I recall the happy and joyous red-coloured days that have since passed us by.'

'Akash, the colour red is the colour of life. It is never abandoned.' Akash loses track of the words, as though he's fumbling around with his fingers, attempting in vain to pick up the Harmonium's tune. The tune begins to play. All of the fingers' veins and sub-veins begin to bleed. Additionally, the heart is bleeding.

'Renu, I think you are currently in Delhi.'

'No, I'm currently located in Sodhpur.'

'Why? I've heard your father-in-law's residence is in Delhi.'

'Yes, you heard correctly. The situation has changed, though.'

'What exactly does that imply?'

'I mean, it's really hard to understand. I have abandoned everything. Our marriage has ended. I'm here now.'

'So, what's about your kids?'

'They don't leave me alone. But there isn't a boy; all three are female.' Renu occasionally used her cloth to wipe the sweat off her brow. Even on that chilly winter night, she was perspiring heavily.

Akash tried miserably to ask, 'How are you?' by holding a deep long breath.

'I'm perfectly fine.'

'What's about your family? What's about your wife and kids?' This time, Akash burst out laughing. 'Renu, where can I locate children? I have not yet married.'

'What? You didn't tie the knot?'

'No.'

'Why?'

'That time was not available.'

Renu looked like she was about to say something, but she didn't. She recalls those day.

'You're not required to say anything about me, Akash.'

'Should I not think about your future?'

'Don't think so. I have parents to take care of me.'

'Then who am I?'

'Who means?'

'Who means who?'

Akash laughed out loud.

Renu has a deep tone to her voice. After removing the husk, she offers Akash two nuts. Akash voluntarily stuffs the huskless nuts into his mouth.

'I have come across your story in a college magazine and read it. You've done a great job with it. But why have you closed the narrative with the song of separation?'

'Hey, you wouldn't get it; it's part of the story's novelty. Happy ending stories elicit a response from the delicate cells of the human psyche. However, don't believe I like it in real life. Let me pass the exam. Then there's the matter of a job. Then....'

'Then what?'

'Marriage.' Akash forcefully shakes her braid. Her lips turn red as she blushes with embarrassment.

'Come on,' Akash says, beaming. The sky has grown gloomy. What a thud all over the place. Storms could occur.

'It rains after the storm, and everything turns green, doesn't it-?'

Akash stared up at the sky with a look of boredom on his face. Now the blue sky is completely dark. How quickly does an avian swarm traverse the sky? What kind of birds are those? The kite is not a migratory bird; instead, it is flying somewhere in search of a home or family.

'Do you recall how we got soaked in the rain that day? I returned home since I was drenched. Then you became ill and had to stay in bed for seven days. So, what occurred to you on that particular day? This is the location where you were expected to arrive. My eyes grew fatigued as I stood there under that tree. You did not come, and you never came again. Why didn't you show up, Akash? Your Renu would not have fallen so early if you had arrived. Her charm would not have faded.'

The sky erupted in surprise. Renu is gazing out the window towards the sky. At dawn, the rays of the sun turn the sky red. Why isn't life more vibrant? Why does regular life seem to fade away?

Renu's nose is filled with the lovely scent of night blossoming Jasmine. The smell fills the chest like a charm, making breathing easier. The shortness of breath is mild. He now appears to have a sway over her physique. She's at a loss for words. Two birds approached and sat on the tin from a distance. Renu glances at him, as if she has no importance in the family and no qualifications to take on any key roles. She is merely a tool for the production of babies. Even so, she was unable to demonstrate adequate production capacity. Three times in a row, the seeds of child production have been sown in Renu's body in the hopes of a son of the child. Unfortunately, she had three daughters on three separate occasions.

'Doctor *Babu*, I assumed I'd be going home with a boy. That didn't happen again. In truth, she is not capable of giving birth to a son. Her mother had only a daughter child as well. I have made a blunder willingly.'

'What exactly are you implying, Arnab *Babu*? Don't you know that when it comes to giving birth to a girl or a boy, girls play a minor role? Only one X is found in the female ovary, while two XY are found in male sperm. A daughter is born as soon as the male X joins the female X. However, if X and Y meet, a boy will be born. This is not the fault of women. What does it mean to be illiterate if you have had an education but do not comprehend it?'

Arnab *Babu* has self-consciousness about him. Having more than one or two children is no longer conceivable, as you are aware. Pay a visit to your daughter. You have a stunning daughter on your hands. Despite his reservations, Arnab *Babu* goes ahead and does it. He took a step closer to Renu's room.

Renu was tending to the infant. When she saw Arnab *Babu*, she lifted her off her lap and placed her on her bed.

'I didn't see this female as expected,' he muttered, slightly annoyed, as he stared at the girl. 'I'm going home with a lovely boy, but I'm having a lot of issues.' Renu's chest trembles and tears well up in her eyes as his final words reach her ears. She gives him a stern look and rebukes him. She looked at him and said in a tone of rebuke – instead of seeing a girl it is better to take rest at home. The wife who repeatedly gives birth to a daughter is again complaining.

'I expected to come home with a boy.' Disgusted, Arnab cast a wide-eyed look at Renu. A deep fear kept gnawing her in the chest like a crab. Renu is ignorant of when the petals of all the flowers of life have fallen one by one. Silently, a muffled breath escapes the chest. Then, floating in the air, she is whisked off into space. As she listens to the constant melody, her mind goes blank. 'Men or women, who came first in the beginning of the world?' What a perplexing question you are asking Renu. 'Men and women do not leave each other alone, but have you ever encountered a naive girl like you?' Renu is embarrassed by her feelings. With a faint smile on her face, she emerges. 'But why are girls treated so badly and humiliated? Why don't they have any respect in the world?'

'Who said women don't have dignity? She is the mother. Motherhood is the ultimate dignity of her life.'

'Only mother, nothing else?'

'What is preventing you? She is a half-sister to her husband. She can devote her entire time to her husband's happiness and suffering. Does this make her life any less fulfilling? After all, the mother is capable of taking such good care of a girl child? Of course, the mother's responsibilities decrease as she gets older. The youngster should then attempt to think in his father's manner. Once he has a bit more maturity, he can also serve as a mother's guardian.'

'How do you come up with ideas like this? Do you have any idea what's going on in the woman's head? In the depths of the mind, there is a current like the Falguni River.'

'All of the girls are making up this gibberish; regardless of who you are, these are your horrible tears, and you are helpless and frail. What sort of prestige are you seeking? What joys, what sorrows? You were brought up in a patriarchal culture. It's important to keep this in mind. I'm not sure why you want to stand up; simply continue to sleep. What will happen if those who inhabit this world do not feel the flames of despair stoked by this meaningless creation?'

'All of us are human. Despite being a woman, you are still a human.' Behind her hands, Renu conceals her face. Her eyes were swollen and red. However, her tears did not fall; instead, they dried up in the harshness of the desert.

Arnab did not return in the evening. He doesn't always return home at night these days. Who knows where he'll end up? Many years have passed, and today, so many years, as well as two lives, are passing in a straight line. They've never met before. It's possible that life is so similar.

How fresh she is when all the flowers first bloom, with a gleam in her eye. Jhilik (flower) covers her four sides with a beautiful aroma, however after a while; the bloom loses its vigour. It starts to loosen up when it loses. The faded body then let go of one flower after another.

'What are you doing standing there? Are the stars of space being tallied when you look up into the sky? Meanwhile, why isn't the call reaching your ears?' Renu's mind is shattered.

Renu takes a step ahead. It seemed as if she had been bound and dragged away by a rope.

'My clothing was in desperate need of a wash. Do it as quickly as possible.'

'Okay.' As the air combines with the air, a deep breath is taken from the chest, and the air gets heavier. Arnab doesn't say much these days, except when it's necessary for work. It's as though everything has gone to sleep. She has become accustomed to it. She can't seem to focus on anything these days. It's as if the brush has stopped moving, and the pen refuses to speak when it comes to writing. She was continuously squandering her time after penning two sentences. If a photograph appeared in the light of a hidden source, yet it is still alive. Arnab's hidden hand, on the other hand, pressed her throat with pride, her eyelids grew damp, and every limb began to wail. Renu's subconscious appears to be floating multiple times. Maybe one day a small wire may slip out of her deep thoughts one by one. Perhaps this is how she will end up lost. Her eyes well up with tears.

The dialogue between Kuntal and Arnab that day still irritates her. 'Kuntal, you get it. If women do not come forward in all the work, then never women's liberation is possible.'

'All right, Arnab *Da*. Your speech that day was very strong. When every female in every house in Bengal walks shoulder to shoulder, equality will arrive. That is something we are looking forward to.'

'I realised there wasn't much left of that day. Women are no longer lagging behind when it comes to starting school. Girls are talented painters and writers, and they have a strong literary spirit. Kuntal, they won't be left behind for long. Furthermore, they are unable to be neglected. Women's backwardness indicates that society is likewise backward.'

'Arnab *da*, you're right. You are exactly right. Through the house of Bengal, we shall attempt to awaken the consciousness of girls.'

'Listen up, Kuntal. Your new generation is a little sensitive. You have little to consider when it comes to judgment from all sides.'

Maya *Di* walks inside the house at that time. 'We were simply talking about you. Kuntal stated that you inspire girls to be self-sufficient and to study. You've also experienced a lot of success.'

'I'm not sure if I'll be successful, but I have no choice but to try!'

'You're heading in the correct way, Maya. Go ahead, but we'll be right there with you. Please don't forget about us.'

'It's not conceivable, so don't mention it. This is exactly what we require: people who are fully aware of their political responsibilities. She then walks over to the kitchen. Renu, whither have you gone?'

'I've arrived. Isn't it still time to eat? Yes, it has been completed. I'm putting the finishing touches on it. Your stories are all over the place, and they're really popular. Only admiration can be expressed. Are you content?'

'Maya *Di*, I don't enjoy it anymore.'

'Maya *Di*, I don't like that anymore. I'm not going to write anything. I will also leave painting. She has also thrown two half-written stories out of the window, claiming that I waste my time by doing so. I can't even get my pictures.'

'No one will throw flowers down your street, but if they can, they will throw thorns. As a result, we must cultivate the mindset of a thorny path walker.'

'I'm no longer able to get on well.' She sobs uncontrollably.

'Listen, Renu, that day is not far away.'

'Maya *Di*, I met you at such a beautiful time, otherwise I would not have been able to survive for so many years.'

'You are making a mistake, Renu. Your power is within you; all you have to do now is waiting for it to awaken.'

'But it has not happened. Day by day I am losing.'

'People who are weak speak in this manner.'

'May be, Maya *Di* is true. The weaker people are always deprived of everything. But not having a son was not her fault. Despite that Arnab could not accept her. Divorce takes places between them. Even if I had accepted her, he would not have been so easily liberated from everything. But what was the benefit of that. This is better than that. He comforts the mind by saying this. Sometimes he calms himself down that way.'

Chapa's two sharp eyes to the side of the nose, she recalls, are pretty appealing. Her tiny face has a weird charm to it.

'Are you here, *Boudi*? During the time of the market, everything is open.'

'Why? Is not your elder brother present?'

'No, I've been ringing the calling bell for a long time, not getting any response I enter into the room. Then I see you are standing here?'

He wraps his clothes around his waist and touches the dishes. A few plates are strewn about at random. At the sound of it, a soft sound comes to Renu's ears. Renu matches herself with Chapa. Chapa, on the other hand, is independent. Has the joy of liberty tinted the petals of his mind? Or, are his eyes worn of despair and exhaustion? Renu couldn't sleep the night after Chapa recounted the story to her.

'I request all of you, not to drive me away. I want to stay with my daughter in the one corner of your porch. I will bring her up on starch. You all please don't drive me away.'

'You must depart; the little child is not ours. You brought her in your stomach.'

'No, no.' Words don't come out of his throat. The tears just keep rolling down.

'Oh, my son, tell your wife to get out of here. Put her daughter in her lap. She and the danger should both flee from here.'

'Mom, where will my daughter and I go? Her eyes haven't fully opened. She has just come to this earth yesterday. Not a day has passed yet. You all should not be so cruel.'

'We do not understand so much. You are bastard. Why should we feed the daughter of someone else? Gourango does not have a daughter who has come out of your womb.'

Chapa is overcome with emotion. She casts a glance at Gourango. Gourango takes a step back and bows his head. Chapa's nose is still filled with the aroma of tuberose.

They haven't even been married a year. Gourango's hand isn't shaking at all today as he tries to shake off that flower. She carefully climbs to her feet and takes the baby into her arms. After that, he marches out of the door. He walks into a tiny slum dwelling near to this perfectly straight railway line. Her parents and two younger sisters still play ekka-dukka in that slum dwelling. Every child does not have to stay in his or her mother's womb for 10 months and ten days – the village's illiterate residents are unaware of this. In 6-7 months, a kid can glimpse the light of the world; – Unaware of this, the uneducated people of the village entangle the lives of countless girls in a false web of stigma that puts their lives in jeopardy.

'*Boudi*, you know – he has remarried and has a son.'

'Are you being jealous, Chapa?'

'No *Boudi*. I wish him happiness. My daughter and I are getting on well. I intend to provide him with a good education. Otherwise, she will suffer in the future, just like I do. Renu's chest felt as though it wanted to let out a long sigh. He tries hard to keep it in and adds that girls need to learn to read and write. You must teach your daughter to read and write.'

'Renu.......' Renu is taken aback by Ram's call. Renu's nose picks up the soft aroma of Renu's cloth's edge. Renu reminds him that he wanted to come that day but did not come. 'This is where we were supposed to arrive that day. We wanted to come under this tree. You, on the other hand, did not show up. You never showed up. Why didn't you show up, Akash?'

'Renu, I never told you. I could not dare tell you. A black mark on my neck is eating away at me for some time. When I discover, my doubt is not unfounded. Believe me; I could not stand before you. Although, doctor has told I would be fine. It is not contagious. Despite that I could not dare tell you. I ran away like a thief.'

Renu says unclearly – 'You are a coward'

The sky is thrilled. A freight train in the distance makes a deafening rumble and proceeds slowly. 'After a long time, seeing you, the pain in my chest begins to ring again, he adds in the manner of peeling nuts. That agony occurred 21 years ago. Far, far away, in the desert of the field, there is a freshly blossomed safflower. Is the sun like this at the end of the afternoon? Akash, look at how strangely the safflower is swinging.'

Akash doesn't say anything, but shakes his head strangely. It comes out of the lips slurred

'Now where have you seen the sun? It's so dark at night.'

'The signal of light is hidden in the darkness, Akash.'

The two are sitting side by side. As if they are sitting side by side on van-rickshaw. The van, which goes at the speed of light over a steep, winding road flanked on both sides by empty fields, transports them slowly into the past. There is nothing but amazement and emptiness for miles. The evening star fades from the sky. It is obscured by dark clouds. The roads will now be inundated once again. The trees will scoop up the shards of darkness on their summits.

****

18

The Ache

Tarik Anowar

Lekha feels a little drowsy while sitting in the waiting room at Howrah Station. Suddenly she opens her eyes hearing her name in a familiar voice. For a while, Lekha realises that she is dreaming. No sooner had she come out of her dreamy illusion than Abhijit pulled a chair and sat down in front of her. Lekha fails to pronounce a single word. For a moment all her words seemed to be lost. Sitting on the chair, Abhijit could not understand how to start the conversation. Finally, Lekha breaks the silence and asks, 'you are here?'

Without answering Abhijit says, 'Lekha, I did not recognize you at first sight when I saw you here today. You look so thin.'

'Yes, to a certain extent, but you too are not like before.'

'Absolutely correct Lekha, time changes everything.'

'That's true.' Lekha replies in a soft voice.

'We have met today after a long gap of ten years but it seems to be only one day. Well, Lekha over the past ten years, have you not ever remembered about the days left behind?'

'Is there any benefit of recalling that now?'

'There may not be any benefit; still, I just want to know.'

'How are you?' Lekha turns aside the context.

'Not well. I am suffering from heart disease.'

'Have you given up smoking?'

'I don't touch cigarette at all now.' Suddenly Lekha becomes oblivious.

'Again, you have lighted the cigarette? Throw, throw it … you will not smoke … I shall leave if you smoke anymore.'

'Well, I will not smoke again.'

'That's a great boy. They both start laughing.'

Abhijit is acquainted with Lekha since their school days. They had been living in the nearby houses. Oneday they discovered that they love each other. Abhijit was a very good football player. One day he got a severe leg injury while playing football. Then he was a second-year student of a medical college. His leg was almost amputated. Of course, his leg was not cut off at last. Lekha had been by his side all day and night for his intensive care in the hospital. Gradually, Abhijit recovered from the injury with the tireless service of Lekha and the good treatment of the doctors.

'Lekha, had you not taken care of me, I probably would not have been able to walk anymore. I don't know how to repay your debt.'

'Is it so easy to recompense the debt? I want to know who will let you allow to repay it? I shall keep you indebted to me throughout your life.' Lekha feels a little embarrassed by saying it instantaneously.

Then one day they got married. Lekha got a job in Delhi. So, they both left Kolkata and moved to Delhi. In a few days they bought a small flat there. Abhijit set up his clinic center and became engrossed in his profession. Within a few days, Abhijit became a popular doctor. Thus, they spent their days very happily. But a gust of wind came from somewhere and extinguished the lamp of their joyous life. Both of them had been undergoing treatment for some days. Lekha had all the criteria to be a mother, but Abhijit lost all hopes to be a father anymore. After receiving the report, Lekha was completely silent by unknown reason. She almost stopped talking to Abhijit. Thus, they passed almost a year in this way.

One evening, Abhijit says, 'Lekha, I'm going out for a while. A patient is in critical condition. Take your supper.'

'Listen, I have something to say.'

'What, can't we discuss it later?'

'That is very important.... Listen, I've been thinking of telling you something for a long time. Our divorce is desirable.'

Abhijit never thought he would hear such things all of a sudden. He stared at Lekha with stupefying eyes for a few moments. Then he slowly lowered his face and said in a calm voice – 'Alright, I agree.'

Then Abhijit hurried out of the house. A deep sob choked his throat.

Returning home that day, Abhijit could not sleep all night. He couldn't even imagine his own existence without Lekha. However, if

Lekha wants, he will definitely divorce her. He always wants to let Lekha stay blessed. But what will happen to him? He has nothing left. Thrusting his head on the pillow, Abhijit sobbed.

After that, Abhijit did not stay in Delhi any longer. He had returned to Kolkata. Even after so many years, he could not forget Lekha for a single day. Occasionally, he feels a throbbing pain in his heart.

'Have you got married, Lekha?'

'Yes.'

'Have you become a mother?'

'No.'

'Why?'

'He passed away within a few months of the marriage. Have you got married?'

'Dad, dad we have completed our shopping.' A five or six years old small girl rushed into the room and stood before Abhijit.

'Dad, look what I've brought for you.' She thumps a big ball in front of Abhijit.

'She is my daughter, Rumki.' Abhijit says taking Rumki in his lap.

'Your daughter?' Lekha says in a befuddled tone.

'Yes Lekha, Rumki is my daughter. I am her father. Some days ago, I have taken all the responsibilities of her and her mother according to judicial law.'

'Can you see your daughter's activity?' A woman arrives with a smiling face and stands beside Abhijit. Lekha has nothing left to understand that she is wife of Abhijit that is Rumki's mother.

'Hurry up! we cannot delay any longer, if it is a little late, we will miss the train. Sujata, now get ready and pack all bag and baggage.' Placing the bag on his shoulder, he hung a large suitcase in his right hand and holds Rumki's hand in his left. From the waiting room Abhijit steps towards the platform. And Rumki's mother with a ladies bag and a hanging bag follows Abhijit. Lekha stares at their movement with fascination. Suddenly, she feels an old ache in her heart, the ache that has been eating her away bit by bit for the last ten years.

****

19

The Witch

Saddam Saikh

If one's foot slips just a little, they risk falling into the pond because of the road's narrowness, which resembles a thin strip. Swapna is therefore moving cautiously. December is characterised by a bitter cold. She has better encircled herself with the blanket. In spite of it, the icy wind tore through her body. The body does not receive enough of the early sun's rays. Swapna enjoys herself so much. Boys leap into the pond while their gowns are on the pond's edge. They swiftly swim around the entire pond. In this frigid winter, don't they feel cold in the pond? The water appears to be ice. What's up with all the people there? By igniting the jute stick, Swapna discovered some people seated in a circle. The majority of them had no clothing on their bodies. So, they are getting ready by warming up. After remaining still for a moment, Swapna begins to stroll away along the pond's edge. An older woman is moving quickly while clutching the market bags and looking at Swapna inquisitively. Sapna right away notices the older woman staring at her. She asks her 'Where are you heading towards Aunty?' Surprisingly the old woman turns to look behind her to see if anyone is nearby. 'I'm asking you', Swapna says with a smile. Then, to Swapna's surprise, the elderly woman asks, 'Who are you? From where are you coming?'

'Where are you going Aunty,' she queries. 'Swapna here. I'm a Kolkata native.'

'Do you hail from Kolkata?'

'Yes.'

'What direction are you travelling in? At which residence?'

I'm not going to anyone's house.

'Then?'

'We, along with many others, have come from Kolkata to join the event taking place at that school.'

'Are you giving a performance there? I mean *Ramlila* or *Nimai Sannas*?'

'No, no, nothing like that.'

Aunty seems to be in a little bit in a hurry. 'Please come, you'll see.'

'I should now go on. I have to go over to the Guru's place, so I don't have time.'

'Where is the Guru's house?'

'That is in *Bamun Para*.'

'Is *Bamun* your *Guru*?'

'Yes – they are our *Guru* for the generation to generation.

'What is there in your bag, Aunty?'

'There is rice inside the bag. For the first time, paddy has been grown in our agricultural area, so I'm giving some rice to our *Guru*.'

'Why don't you eat for yourself before giving the *Guru* rice?'

'What are you referring to? Is it not better for me to give *Guru* rice? The sin committed in a past life is the cause of all sorrow in this life. Therefore, if we give something to *Bamun*, we won't suffer in the afterlife. Then, we would have some happiness. Additionally, we won't have to be born into a lesser caste.'

'Who have you heard this from, Aunty?'

'Why? I learned these from my parents. They claimed that if you work for them, you won't experience any misery. They revered the *Guru* in their day, and they thus instructed us to do likewise.'

'Aunty, is that your paddy field?'

'That is not ours. Does a person in poverty own land? Your uncle is working on someone else's property.'

'Do you have residence in this village?'

'Our house is made of the shed that is next to *Guru's* cowshed.

'Who from your family is with you, Aunty?'

'I have four sons, three daughters and your uncle. All my daughters have got married. My youngest son works at the tea stand while my older and middle sons help their father on the farm. I'm running late because of you. I'll leave now.'

'Aunty, before you move over, would you just listen to me? *Gurudevs* are not trustworthy or honest people. They deceive you and induce false dreams in you. Donating them will be useless, so you should take this quantity of rice back to your house instead. You won't continue to be underfed then.'

'Are you telling me to go back home with my rice? Have you gone insane? Out of backlash, she confronts Swapna. 'Please refrain from saying what you just said, or your tongue will be chopped off. Do you ignore *Bamun*? What I've heard is that we are suffering from unknown sins. You lack any sense of shame. Anywhere you choose, you can move. After gaining some knowledge, you have led the entire nation astray.'

'Ghona's mother, what has happened to you?' Malti walks over to stand by Aunty.

'What will happen? I was informed by the girl that giving food to our *Gurudevs* would not be beneficial. She instructed me to come back with my rice. Malti, would you kindly inform me of the procedure for returning the rice intended for *Gurudevs*?'

'Are you actually bringing rice back with you? The result of this will be starvation in our village. Regarding crop output, everyone will be impacted, not just you.'

'Where are you coming from,' Malti asks Swapna as he peers at her.

'I'm from Kolkata.'

'Why are you in this place? Which home are you heading to?'

'I didn't go to anyone's home. I'm just aimlessly strolling. We've arrived at your school.'

'Why have you begun saying those things here, though? You talk about such things in Kolkata, please. We, the villagers, cannot understand those things.' There quickly gathers a large number of people. Swapna is being watched by everyone. By pointing their fingers at Swapna, people are saying her dreadful things. Swapna is thus terrified. Her throat is already parched. Something absurd caught Swapna's attention in their eyes and faces.

'What has occurred? Why is this place so crowded?' Sonatan advances by pushing through the crowd.

'Please note that this girl has started babbling rubbish in our neighbourhood. She has used derogatory language to describe our *Gurudevs*.'

'What? What are you discussing, Aunty?'

Everyone is telling collectively –Not only these sinful acts to utter but also to hear. Then, in a fit of wrath, Sanatan approaches Swapna. His face and eyes both reflect the spooky attitude. Then, in a grave voice, he asks, 'You came to the school grounds for the meeting, but why are you here?'

Holding her head down, Swapna says, 'I've come here only to visit.'

'It's okay that you're out visiting, you ought to have come back after your visit. Why did you tell Ghona's mother those things?'

Sonatan prevents Swapna from speaking and warns the general public that criticising *Gurudevs* is a kind of sin. This critique of the *Gurudevs* could be harmful to Gona's mother. According to Sonatan, there is no way of knowing what would transpire in the life of Ghona's mother. They will now lose whatever they previously obtained for their survival. As much as he could, Sonatan exudes seriousness in his voice. 'What will happen to us,' Ghona's mother shouted out in fear and asked Sonatan?

'What will occur? You will be cast into hell in the next life. I have no other ideas besides this. Who will refuse it when the suffering of hell has been engraved in your luck?' Standing beneath the tree, Madhav Thakur has been observing the situation for a while. His dreadlocks have been kept in a knot. He also has an extremely lengthy beard. The sacred thread is hanging under his armpit as he dons lungi and dhoti. He's put on his shoes. The people refer to him as Madhav Ghosai and have great respect for him. The crowd has gathered as they watch him advance. Madhav Ghosai has intervened and demanded to know what has taken place. Why is there such a large crowd? He then turned to look at Ghona's mother and questioned her, 'Why are you crying, Ghona's mother?'

'Thakur, please save me; everything is in ruins. My life has been destroyed by this devil.' With a pointed finger, she declares, 'According to Swapna, *Gurudevs* are useless and hypocrites.' 'Why did you listen to her comments while standing here' – Madhav Ghosai asks Ghona's mothers as he places his hand on her shoulder. 'Shouldn't you have left at that point?'

'Was there a way to escape?' Ghona's mother asks while wiping away her tears with her left hand. 'Swapna came in my way.'

'What else is left for you to do? Prepare to enter hell.' 'What will happen to me?' – cries Ghona's mother as she begins to sob. 'Don't cry, Ghona's mother, there is a provision in everything,' Madhav Ghosai croons. 'If you make amends, everything will be well.' The mother of Ghona inhales deeply and lets out a sigh of relief. She cries no longer.

'Will atoning for her sin result in forgiveness?'

Madhab Ghosai shakes his head and replies, 'Yes. It's rather expensive, though. Are you willing to take it on?'

'Sure, Ghosai.' The mother of Ghana hadn't seen her kid in a while. With the sound of her son's speech, her eyes are now glowing. 'Ghona, where do you obtain your money?' she queries.

'Mother, you don't think about it. Right now, I'm planning to sell the brass jug.' Then turning to Madhab Ghosai, Ghona uttered, 'Thakur, what does atonement involve?'

Ghosai had been anticipating this for a very long time. 'Not like that you merely need to spend 200 rupees'

'200 rupees?' This time, he grew terrified and pleaded, 'Won't be a little less, Thakur?'

'There is nothing less than this, right? Is it accurate to say that the cost of purification won't be slightly higher? If you're going to mention this so much, give ten rupees less.'

Swapna didn't get a chance to go because everyone had gathered around her. She seemed to be worn out.

In a severe tone, Madhav Thakur commands, 'Tie the girl to the tree. How can the girl talk like that if she isn't a witch? Stay with her. She will be offered in this sacrifice, which will be performed in front of her.' When Swapna realises there is no way out of the situation, her eyes well up with tears, and her whole body goes cold.

On orders from Madhav Ghosai, Ghanram and Sanatan advance towards Swapna. – Ghanram shouts, 'Satanic! You don't have a place to perform such a repulsive task. Do you really want to damn my mom to hell? Oh you, witch!'

Swapna became frightened as Swapna's hands quickly encircled her back. Her fear of certain death now causes her chest to begin to shake. She has consistently read these news articles in newspapers.

What a heinous event. She had never anticipated seeing that today. Everyone in this room sees her as a witch, thus nobody will want to listen to her. She misses her parents and younger brother a lot as she prepares to face her unavoidable death. She said nothing to anyone when she first entered the streets of this village. 'By this time, everyone must have eaten their lunch. Prosenjit will surely try to find her at least once. He can't possibly know that I'm snared in this trap, can he? He still needs to hear from me a lot more. There is a chaotic situation inside the head.'

The penance is carried out from noon till the afternoon. The mantra is being recited aloud by Madhab Ghosai. In front, there is a fire. In front of the flames stands Ghona's mother. It appears as though the fire is purifying her. The villagers are anxiously awaiting its outcome.

This time, Madhav Ghosai gave Ghana's mother the bowl of excrement and lime and instructed her to consume it while kissing it. Wide-eyed, Ghana's mother regarded the food. It seems as though he will magically finish everything he eats in a flash. Everyone was a little frightened when the Pabitra and the Kamol arrived at that point.

Pushing their way through the maze of people, Pabitra and Kamol enter. Their attention is drawn to the comatose and defenceless Swapna. 'They're going to cause another accident,' claims Kamol. Without waiting a second, Pabitra approached Ghosai and asked, 'What's going on here?' Madhav Ghosai declared the girl to be a witch while scowling and sipping his beverage. She intended to ruin Ghanram's mother.

'So, you bound her!' As soon as they finish speaking, they advance on Swapna. Her chains are released, and her eyes start to get watery. Swapna eventually opens her eyes. Pabitra says, 'You appear to be coming from City. So why are you here?' After hearing everything from Sopna Pabitra had to tell what trouble would have occurred today! Swapna observes them. Her lips begin to tremble in terror.

Both Pabitra and Kamal are college students. The residents of their village both respect and fear them. Nobody would ever want to stop them, then.

Pabitra promises, 'I'll get you there. They're most likely to considering you. For a very long period, that schoolhouse served as our home.' The silence was terrible to Swapna's ears. The day's events spun around her, making everything seem like a nightmare. There was nothing else she could think of. Her perception is that she is to blame. It was improper to show up without letting anyone know. Swapna awakens at the touch of a familiar hand approaching from behind. 'Where have you gone, Swapna? Early in the morning, you vanished. What is the issue? What happened to you?' Pabitra informs Swapna that she needs some rest because she is exhausted before responding.

Prosenjit is now staring in amazement at Pabitra and Kamol. 'What is going on? It seems like everything is crazy. You are who?'

'We are the offspring of this pitiful village. He is Kamol, and I am Pabitra.' Many people are remarking that Pabitra and Kamol did not fare well at all from a distance. It was improper to let the witch go free. The final phrase catches Prosenjit's ear. Where the witch is and what exactly are they saying? Prosenjit had fear and trepidation in his gaze. Pabitra says subtly, 'Here, she is with us.'

'What are you saying?'

'Yes, I'm correct. In the dream-city of this society, such a terrible tragedy would have happened if we hadn't arrived in time.'

'They are who?'

'They are our parents, siblings, and other family members.'

****

20

Friend

Tarik Anowar

Ratna grabbed Keya's hand from behind.

'Hay, Keya when did you come from America?'

Taken aback, Keya turns back and finds Ratna.

'Ratna, you? How are you?'

'Good. You have become so fat and fair, it's very difficult to identify you as compared to the previous Keya.'

'Is it so? What's about you? What's going on nowadays? Are you doing any job?'

'Now, I am teaching in a college. What are you doing?'

'I am also teaching in a school there.'

'I think you are here for some days?'

'Yeah, I have come on two months leave. Almost fifteen or sixteen days I have already passed. Why don't you come one day at my father-in-law's residence?'

'Sure, I will. I could not still meet your husband.'

'How is it possible? You didn't attend our marriage ceremony.'

'Keya, I am really sorry for that. Actually, I had to go to Delhi for an urgent task. I guess you have a daughter, haven't you?'

'Yeah, now she is three years old.'

'O my God! Then you have become a full-fledged household woman, what do you say?'

'Is there any way to escape it? The daughter is too naughty.'

Keya looks at her watch and seems to be a little busy. 'Oho we are too late in our conversation. Who knows whether the girl is crying for not seeing me? Let me go. But you must come…..'

She spoke it glibly to Ratna.

'Of course, I will go.'

Keya walks a few steps forward in order to depart and then comes back again towards Ratna. 'Oho, I haven't given you the house address of my father-in-law. You have to come, ok?'

'Ok, give it to me.' Keya brings out a pen and paper from the bag.

'Listen Keya, you don't have to write the address now. Just pen down the phone number only. I'll ask you the address by phone.'

Keya writes down the phone number and gives it to Ratna. Then she says – 'don't lose the number again. Good bye.'

Keya then gets lost in the crowd. Ratna stares at her for a while. Keya recalls some childhood memories and the days of milk and honey of her youth.

Keya's mother Mayadevi teaches in a high school in Central Kolkata. After losing her husband, she had to struggle very hard in her life with her one-year old daughter Keya. Unsurprisingly grief was her lifelong companion. She was with her husband only for three years. Her father-in-law too died shortly after their marriage. Her mother-in-law passed away before their marriage. So Mayadevi had to manage everything all alone. She admitted Keya in a boarding school for her study. Keya also studied in Vishwa-Bharati University. She was always a meritorious student. After completing her Master's degree, Mayadevi arranged Keya's marriage with Debobrata. Debobrata then just got a job after completing his Engineering course. His father Aniruddho was a Bank Officer. After his retirement, Aniruddho *Babu* permanently settled in Salt Lake. He could not build a house as he had to travel outside Kolkata. Suddenly Debobrata's mother died of a stroke case. He now lives alone in such a big house in Salk Lake. Manik is the only one to stay as his partner. He now takes care of Aniruddho *Babu* and he is the only companion.

Today Aniruddho *Babu* is not physically and mentally well. He comes to the Lake by a Taxi. He has been getting bored in his life for some days. Aniruddho *Babu* sits down on an empty bench nearby. Today, he feels very tired. The setting sun still throws its golden light over Lake's water. It is as if an invisible hand has spread over the sky. It is as if his breath was getting stuck in the crowd around him. Under this circumstance, all the events of distant past start floating in his mind. The memories are both painful and pleasant. Aniruddho loses himself in his childhood memories. In his childhood, Aniruddho had an intense desire to become a policeman. He wanted to catch thieves by chasing with a stick in his hand. A strong feeling of heroism would thrill him. Today Aniruddho *Babu* smiles standing at the last stage in his life. He laughed a little louder. People love to imagine about their past. What is past is past and never comes back. He feels a strange pain in the core of his heart.

'Aniruddho, let's go for a walk to the lake. In the past, you and I used to escape the class lectures….'

'Madhuri, do you remember that day?'

'What do you think? I remember very well. That day Madhuri had dressed herself well. She looked very nice. She would tell me where to sit. There is no empty bench anywhere.'

'Really Aniruddho there is not a little lonely zone by the lake for sitting.'

'Let's go there and sit on the grass.' Aniruddho gently pulls the fringe of Madhuri's Sari. It seems a little awkward thing on that day. The life is very strange, it does not follow any rule.

'*Babu*, will I give you hot tea?' An 18- or 19-years old boy comes with a kettle and stands behind him. Now he comes back to reality from his imaginary world.

'Tea? You would like to give me? Ok, give me a cup.'

He finished the whole in a single sip. Then he took money out of his pocket and paid the price of it.

It is almost evening. A little earlier Manik has closed the door and windows of Aniruddho *Babu's* room. In the evening there are mosquito infestation around. The door and windows cannot be kept open otherwise mosquitos will enter inside. A large number of malaria patients are seen around. Dengue fever too has broken out. Manik is very worried about his master. Aniruddho *Babu* has a habit of studying books.

'*Babu*, let me draw the mosquito net, then you will study inside it.'

'No Manik, I will not go inside the mosquito net now. Bring for me the easy chair to Veranda; I would like to sit there for a while.'

'No *Babu*, the breeze is cold enough to make you chill. Better you go inside.' Nevertheless, he has to follow Manik's words.

All the windows and the door of the room are properly closed. Still, it seems that the cold wind is getting inside from somewhere. It is noticeably cold weather in Kolkata this winter. In his retired lifestyle, Madhuri is not there either. She is gone and will never return again. In fact, Madhuri will not be able to return from there if she wants to. No one can ever do so.

Now, the days seem too long for Aniruddho. The sluggish body gradually becomes burdensome for him. The red coruscation of the setting sun has made a part of the western horizon strangely enchanting. Aniruddho *Babu's* eyes are fixed on that side.

'Come back from the office a little early today.'

'Why?'

'Have you completely forgotten that today marks the second anniversary of our marriage?' Aniruddho says jokingly – 'Who told you that I will go to the office today?'

'You will not go to office?'

'No. listen, pack up your clothes, the car will arrive at nine o'clock.'

'What do you mean?'

'That means we will go to Digha.'

'What? Why didn't you tell me before? And just before two hours you are saying the car is about to come?'

'It was a surprise for you.'

There was a hurly burly situation that day. Madhuri forgot many things to take in hurriedly. But she didn't forget to take Aniruddho's favourite camera.

Neither there is any boat nor raft under his feet now. His life is flowing on the floating-wood, which sometimes floats, sometimes sinks and sometimes lost in the deep current. Is there nothing new to happen now? Yet nothing brings to an end to a human being. He courageously follows the old path with new hopes in his heart. He imagines all these things in his mind.

'*Dada*, may I get a cigarette?' He did not notice when someone came and sat next to him.

'Cigarette? No, I don't smoke.'

'You do not smoke?' The man looks at him in surprise. There is a mark of annoyance in his face. 'Why don't you smoke? It is the only cheap food left for us. We smoke....' then the man went away muttering something.

Aniruddho takes a good look at the man. He appears to be thirty years old. But why is he wandering around like this? The man seemed to be educated. Is he then unemployed? Is he exhausted of looking for a job? Is it like falling of a sprout bud? But why? Why is such anarchy? Who is responsible for this? It is as if the shadow of inauspicious cloud gradually engulfed the whole world.

It is raining heavily all day. Everyone is locked in the house. From distance, the forest looks like the turbulent waves of the sea which is dancing at great intensity with the rhythm of the wind. And the gigantic waves of the sea strike the coast with the roar of thunder. The couple capriciously move forward on the lonely beach where the silver waves are crashing. They could not realise when they were enchanted by the cold wind of the sea under the palm trees. A mysterious peace spells over the body and mind. Aniruddho tightly grabs Madhuri's hand. She moves a little closer. Both seem to be lost in the eternal current.

Aniruddho *Babu* suddenly wakes up from his utopia due to the cold breeze. He sees that the gathering of the people by the lake has been dwindled away. At some distance, a few couples are sitting scattered. Aniruddho *Babu* looks at his watch. 'Oho! It's nine o'clock? The night has befallen so early me suppose? Manik must be worried at home. There is still a person in this world who governs me.'

Debobratahas returned to the country after five years. Keya too has come with him. They have come only for two months. The day is cloudy since morning. For the entire day, the sun has just once showed its face then hidden behind the clouds. It is almost afternoon but the sun is still invisible. It looks like silence has fallen over all around. The wind has also stopped blowing. It seems there will be a torrential rain.

'Rain in winter, Keya it will be very cold today.' Debobrata wrapped himself with a shawl.

'Listen.' Keya comes and stands beside him.

'What, are you telling me something?'

'Yes, come. I have been thinking of telling you something for few days.'

'Yes, tell me.'

'But that is very important…...'

'Ok.'

'Debobrata, Dad lives here alone and there is no one to look after him except Manik.'

'Why, your mother visits him often?'

'Yes, she comes. But what I wanted to tell......'

'What?'

'Since Dad is not willing to go to America with us, I think we should make arrangements so that he could stay here better?'

'As your choice. Who prevents you?'

'But Debobrata that is not an easy task.'

'Why? Why not easy?'

'Listen, how it will be if Dad remarries?'

'Dad's Marriage! Are you crazy? Keya, is it possible?'

'Why not possible? Now Dad is old enough, he needs someone intimate to take care of him and accompany him with love and affection. Moreover, Dad is alone; he needs a partner. Over all, a close friend.'

'What nonsense are you saying?'

'Listen Debobrata! Dad is here all alone. There is no one to care him properly. We live in America which is very far away. We can never be with Dad. There is no one here to talk with him except Manik. This loneliness will dwindle if Dad remarries. Besides, we don't really feel good being far away from him.'

'Who will marry this 60-year-old man?'

'I shall fix the bride. Just tell me, do you agree?'

'What if I agree? Don't you need to take Dad's consent?'

'Leave that responsibility to me.'

Keya puts her head on the pillow and closes her eyes. The sound of Calling-bell wakes her up. Tusi has been very naughty nowadays. She interferes with every little thing. There is no sleep in her eyes. After many pursuits, she just falls asleep. Tusi's one hand is on Keya's body, she just gently removes Tusi's hand on the pillow next to her. Tusi moves a little in sleep. There is no one in the house. So, Keya goes and opens the door.

'Come inside. Is it time now for you to come? You wouldn't have found me here any longer if you had delayed even one more day.'

'Why? Are you going tomorrow then?'

'Yes,' showing sofa, Keya says, 'please sit down.' Striding a little towards the door, she called Manik loudly.

'Yes, *Bou-muni*?' Manik hurriedly appears before her with a towel on his shoulder.

'Give us two cups of tea. And some sweets are kept in fridge, bring them on a plate.'

'Keya, I don't eat sweets of fridge. My teeth cannot bear cold foods. And you know better that l don't like sweets.'

Pushing the curtain, Manik entered into the room. On a large plate in his right hand, there are few *Luchis* and *Ghugni* in a pot, and a glass of water in his left hand.

'Put it on the table there.'

'*Bou-Moni*, Shall I bring another plate for you?'

'No, I will not eat.'

Ratna picks up the water glass and suddenly it slips down from her hand.

'O shit! I have increased your trouble.' Ratna bends down for picking up the broken pieces of the glass. Keya promptly grabs her hand. 'Stop it, your hand may cut off. Manik will clean it soon. Please go and wash your hand in the basin faucet.'

Ratna moves towards the basin and says, 'Keya, where is your husband? Call him, l want to meet him.'

'He has gone to market for purchasing something.'

'So bad luck! Then there is no possibility of meeting him again. Good bye!'

'Look they have come back.'

As soon as the door opens…..they enter with a load of things in their hands. Ratna looks at Keya's mother in astonishment. She indistinctly says – 'What! Is this Aunty, vermilion on your head and *Shakha Pola* in your hand?'

'Are you surprise to see my mother?'

'Ratna, my mother is all alone. Her loneliness troubles me a lot. Today, I can go to America in peace. I have been helped a lot in this regard by Debobrata, my husband.'

****

21

The Crossing

Saddam Saikh

Sagar, Kajori, and their son Dickie manage to get into the train after pushing their way through the crowd. Sagar glances around to see if there is any place to sit, but there isn't. 'Give the baby to me,' an elderly gentleman asked as they stand in the middle of the seats on both sides. The old man takes the child from Sagar's lap and sets him down on his own. Despite his unfamiliarity, Dickie doesn't say anything. He is peacefully sitting on his lap. Kajori takes Dickie when two seats in Durganagar become available. The man glances at Dickie with a beautiful smile on his face. Dickie drifts off to sleep as the chilly wind blows outside the window. The train keeps on, occasionally stopping briefly at a station. 'Gyanabilas, I could not have imagined meeting you today in this way.' The gentleman in front of him and another gentleman alongside him are conversing cheerfully.

'I'm truly stunned to see you. But Akhilesh, you've undergone a lot of change.'

'It's only a matter of time before it happens. Change is inevitable as we grow older. Though you look familiar but I am hesitant to speak. My skepticism vanishes after holding a conversation with you.'

'Akhilesh, the smudge at the base of your sideburns helped me recognise you. Is that right?' They both burst out laughing.

With a smile on his face, Gyanbilas remarks that he vividly recalls his childhood days.

'I also remember. People at this age are haunted by their past. The past is the elixir of youth. Do you have any memories of Shyamalima from your youth?'

'Of course, I remember.' He inwardly says how he can be forgotten! 'Here I am, still wandering aimlessly through my life.' Gyanbilas takes a big breath and exhales it.

'My next meeting is on Tuesday, for sure,' says Shyamlima.

'Well.'

'You won't tell me anything?'

'What should I say?'

'But anything?'

Gyanbilas comprehends what Shyamalima is saying. However, because he is the oldest brother's son in the household, he is powerless, and the circumstance isn't much better. His parents have a lot of hope for him. He is presently a college student. Nothing has yet been thought of. The mind wants him to be something he is not capable of. Despite Shyamalima's best efforts to hide them, tears were streaming from her eyes. At the time, Gyanbilas was unaware that Shyamalima was still alive in his heart.

'Did you get married, Gyanbilas?'

'No, I'm not married.'

'Tell me, then, the stubbornness not to get married is not over yet, right?'

'You have a son, don't you say Gyanbilas.'

'No two boys.'

'What are they doing now?'

'They are doing government jobs.'

'Then your family is full-fledged, isn't it?'

'If you don't get married, you don't know, so what is family all about Gyanbilas? You remained like a child for the rest of his life.'

'I'm not married, but my niece and nephew grew up with me. My niece got married. Nephew is studying engineering. I built a home at Salt Lake a while ago. My family is no less. Now it's life after retirement. Yet there is no one to look after them. Sister and brother-in-law passed away in a scooter accident. It's been several years. With them, life is going on. My niece sometimes comes to visit me. She is very strict. She has made it sure of my food list of my food habits. My son-in-law comes often to take care of me and calls several times a day.' It feels good thinking of their careful restriction but in this age their restriction does not affect Akhilesh. Taking a packet of cigarettes from his pocket Gyanbilas smiles and says, 'there is no niece rule now therefore bought four packets of cigarettes.' He took out a cigarette from the packet and handed it to Akhilesh. He also takes one. Hold on to the cigarette lips Gyanbilas gives lighter to Akhilesh and then lit his cigarette and says, 'smoking with pleasure I am prohibited to smoke. My niece strictly looks after that. If she ever sees me smoking, she will turn everything upside down. Look what I am doing – talking about myself only. Is your son married?'

'Just marriage? I have a grandchildren's family.'

'Where did you build your home?'

'I didn't build a home. I rent in Dumdam junctions. I used to do teaching in primary school. How much more did I get paid for it? After doing a few private tuitions I somehow managed to educate them. After retiring, I got two lakhs. I divided the money between the two of them thinking that post retirement life would pass with ease. But fate did not accept it. The two of them shared an amount and also shared us like money. The two of us left with them like two pieces of furniture.'

'Dad, your one month will be completed tomorrow, and you have to go tomorrow. Arnab will return from the office tomorrow. You should be ready.'

Akhilesh hesitated a little but pushed out the secret pain of his mind. 'I haven't seen your mother for a long time, my eldest son – let me stay for tomorrow'…before he finishes his talk Abhishek says, 'no, who else will take you.'

'I will leave alone the day after tomorrow, you don't have to go,' says Akhilesh in a tired tone.

'No, you don't need to do that. Tomorrow Arnab will come; with him you will go. Think over it – you are getting older. You should not take the risk of travelling alone.'

'Then bring your mother after two days.'

'No, no, it's not possible, Dad. Both I and Moyna go for work. Who else will look after Tuski? Don't emphasise on it. Mother is perfectly well. You can talk over the phone, can't you?'

'Phone? She can no longer be seen with the naked eye,' says Akhilesh indistinctly.

'Hello, who is there?'

'I am talking.' They left for the office.

'I am saying, did they leave for the office?'

'Yes, that's it.'

'What are you doing now?'

'I'm tidying up the kitchen, what are you doing?'

'I am getting ready to go for a bath.'

With deep feeling he asks 'how are you? Do you have any problems? Are you taking medicine on time?'

'No, no, you don't think about anything, I'm fine, I'm fine.'

'I haven't seen you for a long time Lavanya; I want to see you very much.'

'I want to see you too.'

'Do you know Lavanya, the little boy of our eldest son has become very naughty, and if you come you can see just like the little boy like the eldest son in childhood.'

'Is that so?'

'Yes, then what am I talking about? My daughter-in-law takes great care. Don't let me touch him at all. It is the precaution if I touch the small child with dirty hands, that's it. Infections can occur.'

'They are today's generation children; their care must be different. But here my oldest daughter-in-law leaves Tuski with me. They have their office. I bathed Tuski and sent her out to school. The school bus comes in front of the house. The oldest daughter-in-law, of course, has given me all the responsibility. I even have to tidy up their kitchen as I also have to look after what Roma, the cook, cooks for us. I even have to tidy up their tiffin. So, I don't have time to take a light breath in the morning.'

'It's like this only whatever you are saying. I also have the responsibility to send her to school when I stay there. But there is one more thing to take her by the hand in the evening that you don't have to do.'

'No, of course I do. I sometimes take her for an evening walk. Otherwise, she bet with me on as you usually take her to walk. I, of course, sit on the front bench of the park. Tuski plays with her friends.'

'Listen to me, put your dirty clothes in one place and I'll wash and iron them.'

'When will I get those?'

'Why, you will come back in a month, then you will wear them.'

'Okay.' A muffled sigh comes out of Akhilesh's chest. Lavanya feels it. 'All will be well in time.' says Lavanya by removing the tear-soaked throat.

Akhilesh's throat tightens. He puts down the phone. It's been raining all day. It has been raining since yesterday. Today, its incidence seems to have increased a lot. Frequent lightning flashes with the roar of the clouds. Occasionally there is a gust of wind blowing through the windows and doors. Akhilesh is sitting on the sofa with the windows and doors closed. It's a little cold. He pulls a thin sheet and puts it on. Dirty clothes are packed and left in one corner of the room. The details of his nomadic life are in his bag. Again, if the bag is too heavy, the eldest one gets angry. 'If you are going for a month, what is the point of making the bag so heavy? Is there? Can't fill a little less?'

Akhilesh heard the calling bell and walked towards the door. As soon as the door opened, Arnab entered the room.

'Dad, are you ready?'

'You're so wet little son, change your pants.'

'No, Dad, I have to go home soon. Otherwise, she will be in deep thinking.' Barasat local enters the Durganagar station making noises. 'Give me the bag dad. You get up first.' All the trains on the Bonga line are very crowded. However, it is a little less crowded as it is in Barasat. Somehow Arnab Akhilesh was able to get on the train pushing the crowd. But no one goes inside, everyone is everywhere as the door is opened and wind is blowing. Nobody goes inside so there is a lot of pressure on the door. Akhilesh tries hard to get inside.

A young man stood up and asked him to sit down. Akhilesh felt a little hesitant getting the seat. The train has not been moving for five minutes. Akhilesh knows the reason for not signaling the train crossing with the train going to Sealdah here. The train came and stopped. Akhilesh knows that the train carried his only life partner. He has spent a lot of time in the same house with her. Happiness and sorrow are for those who are involved in life. She is a dream today, just a memory. Why the eldest son and the oldest son have chosen this train for so long. Maybe both of these trains bring us benefits. He himself goes to the oldest son's home by train. He looks out of the window of the train. The face that is recognisable in his eyes, as far as the eye can see, he searches for a similar face with curious interest. Even if he sees, he can get the man he longs for. Their train leaves first, leaving Lavanya on a long journey. Tears come to Akhilesh's eyes. He sits blindfolded, helpless.

'Dad, time has come for us to get off.' Akhilesh gets back to his senses.

'*Chhoto Khoka* in Madhyamgram with the train we passed in the crossing, maybe your mother was in it, isn't it?'

'Yes, she should be on that train.'

'Your mother didn't know that I am sitting on the next train?' Arnab was annoyed by his father's words. This time he said in a threatening tone, 'since then you have been making a fuss, haven't you seen my mother? Many years you have stayed together, why do we now need to split our time between two locations? '

'Nothing like that happened, if the same thing happened in your life, then you can't understand today,' Akhilesh said the words in his mind.

'*Baba*, Oh! Your little boy is very naughty today he may not be able to eat pulses.'

'Why, what happened?'

'He was walking away with a handful of salt on the branch of a boiling pot in a gap, and his aunt saw this. I can't take it anymore; you take care of your son.'

'When he gets older everything will be okay.'

The little boy came from nowhere and ran away and jumped on the lap of his mother, hiding his face.

'Did you see that,' says Akhilesh.

Akhilesh is shaking with the newspaper in his hand. He will be able to feel the taste of liberation for now. Such incidents will happen in his life again. Tears come up in Akhilesh's eyes with joy. Retired teachers of government high schools will be given pension. He repeatedly opened his eyes to see the newspaper. Isn't it a dream? A few words from the newspaper made every pore shiver in the whole body of Akhilesh. They will be able to live together again, Lavanya and Akhilesh. There is a small room and a cot. The rest of life will be spent there well. No one can stop them anymore to stay together. No power will be able to separate them. 'I don't have to plead to my sons. Let me meet with your mother only once. You don't have to tolerate long faces again.' He has not seen Lavanya for the last five years. He doesn't know how she is now. Maybe she is thin now and must have got black spots in the corner of her eye. The hair on the head must have gotten white a little more. Akhilesh is overwhelmed with the joy of freedom. Akhilesh is intoxicated with the joy of new life.

The train arrives at Bangaon station and comes to a complete halt. The train isn't nearly as crowded as it formerly was. 'Gyanbilas,' Akhilesh adds with the suitcase in his hand, 'Come to our place sometime. Your sister-in-law continues to be a fantastic cook. My wife and I live there. Every day, several more people arrive and depart. All of them are my students. With all of them, I maintain a respectful silence. One day, you're welcome to see my new family.' Sagar was completely absorbed in their discussions. He begins to comprehend Kajori's statements. 'Dickie is yours, and I'll take the bags.' Sagar examines Dickie's sleeping face on Kajori's lap. Then he takes Dickie, the sleeping boy, in both hands and caresses his face like a sail. Kajori is in a bad mood. Kajori feels uncomfortable with this unusual behavior of Sagar. 'What are you doing? His raw sleep will be broken.'

****

Voice of a Bengali Dalit Womanist: Conversation with Bengali Dalit Writer Manju Bala

Introduction about the Writer

Manju Bala is a contemporary Dalit voice in West Bengal assumed to be dominated by "Bengali Bhadralok". She is a Dalit feminist writer as well as an activist. She was born into a Bengali Dalit Hindu family in 1948 in Calcutta. Her parents migrated from Bangladesh (erstwhile East Pakistan) to what is now West Bengal in the midst of chaos that prevailed during the partition of colonial Bengal. She obtained her bachelor's degree from University of Calcutta. She has produced a number of books. These are *Osharohir Opekkhai* (Waiting for the Horse-rider), *Churno Somudrer Dhew* (Waves of Shattered Sea), *Chothurtho Bishwer Chitrolekha* (The Portrait of the Fourth World), *Chorabali* (Quicksand), *Uttoran* (The Ascension). She also runs a magazine named *Akhon Takhon* (Now and Then) since 1997 which offers in-depth articles about the struggle of Dalits in fighting the exclusionary upper caste mainstream to find a space for themselves. Her writings are stark in portraying the long ongoing struggles of lower caste Bengali people to gain respect from and acceptance by the upper caste Bengalis. She is the mouthpiece for the lower caste people who are striving to lay claim to a space in a caste-ridden society and calling for the purification of the tainted social system.

Question: Does caste discrimination really exist in West Bengal?

Manju Bala: Yes, it does exist. To substantiate my argument let me put up two evidences.

1. The daughter of my friend took admission in a college in Sanskrit. More often than not she would find herself face to face with an untoward question by upper-caste teachers and fellow mates as to why she got into college with Sanskrit for

she belonged to lower caste background; hence they recognise Sanskrit as the subject of the Brahmins.

2. One day a Brahmin went to a school to get his son admitted in a particular class. One of my friends belonging to a lower caste was a serving as a teacher in that school. Upon entering into the office, the Brahmin told his son to extend the greeting to the teacher by folding his hands maintaining a safe distance from the teacher instead of touching her feet. When the lady teacher advised the students to take her blessing by touching her feet, the Brahmin father snapped out why the student should touch her feet as she belongs to lower caste.

All these evidences bear a witness that the caste system is prevalent in West Bengal. In West Bengal practicing of caste system has taken a different shape in comparison to other states of India. Here the Bhadraloks (gentlemen) instead of inflicting physical torture on the lower caste people they harass them on psychological level.

Question: Take us through your childhood period experiences?

Manju Bala: I never felt my childhood; it seemed to me that I grew up too early. The place where my father was appointed as a teacher was inhabited by lower caste people especially the Santhals. They were in the stern grip of abject poverty. They would raise pigs and other domestic animals for their livelihood. I had witnessed their hardships how they would meet their ends meet. My father extended his helping hand to these impecunious people. Sometimes they would run out of foods. Thereby they would satisfy their hunger by boiling the roots of nymphaea nouchali. I would frequent their houses and feel their pains and suffering. Since my childhood I have observed that my parents are not used to worshipping as they think that it is the culture of Brahmins.

Question: Whom should we address as Dalits in India?

Manju Bala: To clarify the term 'Dalit', I would like to take recourse to the ancient history of Indian continent. Nomadic invaders Aryans were the ancestors of today's Brahmins. These worriers Aryans were very advanced in terms of the usage of arms by means of which they took hold of indigenous Indian tribes. The indigenous people who did not give in to the Aryans took refuge in the very remote areas. The Aryan brought in a pecking order in the society by dividing it into four categories on the basis of profession. They put themselves at the top of that hierarchical social structure. Thus, they started to concentrate the whole power of the society in their own hands and rule over the other three lower castes. Those indigenous tribes who did not bow down before the Aryans were proclaimed as untouchables and outcastes. The Shudras belonging to the lowest caste were equally treated like outcastes. The touch, breath, shadow, sound and sight of the Shudras were declared as impure which could easily defile the Brahmins their god and goddesses. Different types of restrictions were imposed on these untouchables and treated inhumanly. These marginalised people are called Dalits in the present day.

Question: How do you look at your identity?

Manju Bala: As I was born in a Dalit family, I look myself on as a Dalit. Thereby I am au fait with the struggles of the survival of my community. And I give vent to their voices in my writing.

Question: When did the Dalit consciousness grow in your mind?

Manju Bala: At a very tender age, Dalit consciousness started to have a grip over me. I have witnessed the people of my community facing caste discrimination in the different strata of the society. The pains and suffering of these people generated the caste consciousness in me.

Question: How have your parents got through the caste discrimination?

Manju Bala: As my parents were economically well-off, therefore they did not experience the harsh discrimination of casteism as the pauperised do. But I have seen how the poor people of my community become the victims of inhuman casteism.

Question: Have you ever found yourself face to face with caste discrimination?

Manju Bala: To be honest, I have not faced stern caste discrimination. But scantily I have experienced it whenever I have been in the company of upper caste friends. My upper caste friends sometimes tell me that I do not look like a Dalit. It indicates that the upper caste people have formed a negative conception about that the Dalits that Dalits are uncivilised.

Question: What is Dalit Literature according to you?

Manju Bala: It is the literary writings by the Dalits for the Dalits with their Dalit consciousness. This literary domain was initially developed in Maharashtra by the thoughts and ideals of Babasaheb Ambedkar. Thereafter this literary trend was gradually spread in different vernaculars in different parts of India. The prime objective of this literature is to fight against the cruel caste system and to form a casteless society.

Question: Please tell us something about the Bengali Dalit literature?

Manju Bala: Bengali Dalit literary movement was started in 1992 in the aftermath of the sad demise of Chuni Kotal, a tribal girl from Lodha community. This literature took root in West Bengal with the publication of Chothurtho Dunia, a Dalit literary journal in the year 1994.

Question: What led up to the publication of your first book? What made you inspired to be a writer?

Manju Bala: No writer in particular has inspired me to get down to writing whatever I have written. Some experiences and events of my life led up to me writing my first book. Actually, I took up the pen after the deep observation and experiences of the tribulations of my community living in the neck of my woods. I would always have a passion for reading different types of genres but I never thought of writing novels, short stories and the like as my career. Though I got into writing on my own but I was greatly influenced by the ideologies of Dr. Bhimrao Ramji Ambedkar. I set out my literary journey by writing poems and essays which were praised by renowned writer Ranjit Kumar Shikdar, an intimate friend of my father. I entered into the Bengali Sahitya Sanstha (Bengali Literary Organisation) in the end of 1994 with the recommendation Dr Achintya Biswas.

Question: Do you have time to read other Dalit writers? Whose works do you love to read?

Manju Bala: To my opinion, one cannot write well within a genre if he/she does not extensively read the works of that genre. I am used to read a lot and I read a variety of genres. I take time out to go through the works of Meena Kandasamy, Bama, Urmila Pawar, Jatin Bala, Baby Kamble, Anita Bharti, Manoranjan Byapari, P Sivakami, Omprakash Balmiki, Daya Pawar and the others.

Question: You have set out on your writing journey as a female Bengali Dalit writer. It has a particular parameter as to the subject matter and you are passionate about that. Do you ever feel smothered about that particular subject matter?

Manju Bala: I have never felt the subject matter as confining for me. Whatever I write is the outburst of my pent-up angst the rigidity of caste hierarchy prevalent in our society. Through my writing I resist against the subordination and oppression of Dalits Schedule Castes (SC) belonging to the lowest rung of caste hierarchy at multiple levels by the people who are on the upper scale of hierarchy. Therefore, I never I feel it difficult to write within a strict guideline of this subject matter and I feel purged staying true to it.

Question: How do you differentiate yourself as a Dalit female writer than the male Dalit writers?

Manju Bala: Patriarchy has a sway over almost every stratum of the society and Dalit community is not out of the purview of the society. The Dalit male writers generally portrait the common issues of the Dalit community as a whole. But the Dalit female writers alongside the normal issues also minutely focus on the woman issues. Dalit women are double oppressed as a Dalit as well as a Dalit woman. They are victimised inside and outside of the house. Dalit women are sexually harassed by the upper caste men at the workplaces. I have specially emphasised the women issues which have been overlooked by the male Dalit writers.

Question: Please tell us briefly about your writings?

Manju Bala: I have tried to touch on different genres. I have composed two books of poetry – *Osharohir Opekkhai* (Waiting for the Horse-rider) and *Churno Somudrer Dhew* (Waves of Shattered Sea); a book of essays – *Chothurtho Bishwer Chitrolekha* (The Portrait of the Fourth World); a book of short stories – *Chorabali* (Quicksand); and a drama – *Uttoran* (The Ascension). All my writings revolve around the Dalit issues.

Question: What was the condition of the Dalits in past and how they are in present in Bengal?

Manju Bala: Yes, there is a change. Earlier in Bengal the lower caste people were known as Chandals (those who work in the crematorium) an abusive term. They were treated as untouchables by the so-called educated *Bhadralok* (gentle) people. They had to live outside of the city. Agriculture, fishing and boating were their main source of livelihood. Now in the post independent India with the implementation of the constitution the condition of their lives is uplifted to some extent. Now they are in political, administrative and other different sectors. But the caste hatred mentality is still visible among the Bengali *Bhadralok*. They cannot bear to see the progress of scheduled caste community. Even today we see the Bengali lower caste people face caste discrimination in different ways.

Question: What is basic difference between African-American black woman writers and Indian Dalit woman writers?

Manju Bala: Yes, there are some similarities and dis-similarities between the two. The black women and Dalit women are both doubly oppressed. The black women suffer from colour and gender discrimination whereas the Indian Dalit women suffer from caste and gender discrimination.

Question: Would you tell us something about Dalit feminism?

Manju Bala: The female Dalit writers like Bama, Urmila Pawer, Kalyani thakur and me are fighting against caste and gender discrimination through our writings. The mainstream feminists hardly highlight the issues of the Dalit women. So, we Dalit female writers are trying to give vent to the lament of women of the Dalit community.

Question: Is there any difference between Bengali Dalits and the Dalits residing in the other parts of India?

Manju Bala: Yes. The Dalits in Maharashtra and Tamil Nadu are more oppressed than the Dalits residing in West Bengal.

Question: Please tell us something about Matua movement?

Manju Bala: Matua religious movement was started by Harichad Thakur and his son Guruchand Thakur as a protest against inhuman treatment meted out to them by the orthodox Brahmins. This religious movement was greatly influenced by Buddhism. Their main mottos were neither to follow the commands of Brahminical scriptures nor to follow their cultural and social traditions. Prior to the partition of Bengal their main center was in Faridpur in

Bangladesh and after partition the center shifted at Thakur Nagar in South 24 Parganas in West Bengal.

Question: Tell us something about the involvement of Matua in politics in the current time?

Manju Bala: The unity that Harichad Thakur and his son Guruchand Thakur created by bringing them together under an umbrella has fallen apart for their entanglement into politics. The different political parties like TMC, BJP and INC have selected their political representatives from them and created a political tension among them. Thus, they have been divided into different political groups and their unity is dismantled. All these happen because of the conspiracy of the Brahmin political leader.

Question: How are Ambedkar's ideas reflected in your works?

Manju Bala: Just as Dr Bhimrao Ambedkar has strived all his life resisting against the caste discrimination and building up equality and brotherhood in the society, in the same way I have tried my level best to tread the path of Ambedkar through my writing.

Question: How mainstream Bengali *Bhadralok* writers portray the Dalits in their writings?

Manju Bala: The Bengali mainstream writers have presented Dalits in their writing in a very derogatory way. They have not shown Dalits as heroic figures. They have drawn them as marginalised ones like labourers, slaves from their sympathetic observation. For example, the Bengali mainstream writer Manik Bandopadhyay in his novel *Padma Nadir Majhi* (The Boatman of the River Padma) was unable to portray the real pains and struggles of the poor fishing community. But the Dalit writer Adwaita Mallabarman minutely delineated in his novel *Titash Ekti Nadir Naam* (A River Called River) the hardship of the community as he would belong to the same community.

Question: Do you foster any repentance for being a Dalit woman?

Manju Bala: To be honest I do not have any repentance as a Dalit, rather I am proud of my identity as a Dalit woman. It aches my heart seeing the people of my community divided among themselves by the ruse of cunning Brahmins.

Glossary

Abir: Brightly coloured powder of a sort thrown into the air and on to others in celebration of the Hindu festival of Holi.

Alu Pocha: Rotten Potato

Baba: Father

Babu: Gentleman, a respected person

Bamun: Upper Cate Bhadralok

Begun Pocha: Rotten Brinjal

Bhadralok: Bengali well-educated and prosperous people

Bolohori Horibol: Chant the name of Hari during funeral

Bordi: Elder sister

***Boudi*:** Wife of an elder brother/ sister-in-law

Bou-muni: A Bengali term that is used to address a daughter-in-law.

Chanral: Bengali Namashudras were earlier known as Chanral

Charanamrita: A sweet drink that is considered as Elixir of Life.

Chhoto Khoka: Youngest son

Da: Generally, means elder brother in Bengali

Dada: Generally, means elder brother in Bengali

Dadababu: Elder brother

Danka: Danka is a Hindustani word. It denotes a sort of a drum huge in size.

Di: Elder sister

East Pakistan: Now it is Bangladesh

Ghugni: Ghugni is a snack, native to the Indian subcontinent, especially popular in Bengal.

Guru: Hindu spiritual instructor.

Gurudev: Hindu spiritual instructor.

Kali: A Hindu goddess

Kantha: A form of embroidery often practiced by rural women

Kulin Brahmins: The Bengali Brahmins who follow Hinduism rigorously are known as Kulin Brahmins.

Luchi: Deep-fried flatbread made of Maida flour

Mansha puja: Hindu snake goddess Manasa is mostly revered in different Indian states primarily for fertility, prosperity as well as the prevention and treatment of snakebites.

Mantrashakti: The power of spiritual words/souds

Naru: Naru or Nadu is a very popular sweet is made from coconut and is very popular in Bengali households.

Nimai Sannas: It is Bengali socio-cultural and religious performance dedicated to Bhakti saint Chaitanya Mahaprabhu.

Paite ceremony: A traditional Indian ceremony called Paite (Thread Ceremony), also known as Upanayana, is used to commemorate the beginning of education in spiritual and other subjects.

Para: Locality

Pishima: Father's sister

Pocha: Rotten

Prasadi Flowers: A type of flower presented to a deity

Puja: In Hinduism puja is worship or ritual performed by Hindus to one or more deities

Rabindra Sangeet: Tagore's songs

Ram Lila: A Festival that is organised during the Dussehra which recalls the battle between Rama and Ravana.

Shakha pola: Shakha pola bangles are shell and coral bangles that are worn by Bengali brides.

Sheetala puja: The seventh and eighth days of the Hindu month are designated as the Sheetala Saptami and Sheetala Asthami, respectively, for the festival of the goddess Sheetala.

Sonar Chamooch: Golden Spoon (Scheduled Caste community is often ironically called as Sonar Chamooch or Sonar Chand (golden moon) as they are entertaining government reservation policy)

Index